G. R. Hamer's newest book, *The Beginnings of Nykloneci*, held me captive from the beginning to the end. As I read each word I felt as if I was part of the story. This story reveals the hidden evil that surrounds our daily lives. As with Nykloneci, the battles we face on a daily basis may or may not be fully recognized. Some battles will be longer than others but the strength we attain from each battle will allow us to win the war. This book allows us to share in Nykloneci's battles against evil. His battles were many, but the love and guidance of family and the protection of a strong leader gave him the weapons needed to overcome the battle within.
—Stella M. Pyles

I really enjoyed this book, and I learned a lot from it, especially about the portals. I'm looking forward to reading the next one.
—Geraldine Humnicky-Murphy

THE BEGINNINGS OF Nykloneci

G. R. Hamer

THE BEGINNINGS OF Nykloneci

TATE PUBLISHING
AND ENTERPRISES, LLC

The Beginnings of Nykloneci
Copyright © 2012 by G. R. Hamer. All rights reserved.

No part of this publication may be reproduced, stored in a retrieval system or transmitted in any way by any means, electronic, mechanical, photocopy, recording or otherwise without the prior permission of the author except as provided by USA copyright law.

This novel is a work of fiction. Names, descriptions, entities, and incidents included in the story are products of the author's imagination. Any resemblance to actual persons, events, and entities is entirely coincidental.

The opinions expressed by the author are not necessarily those of Tate Publishing, LLC.

Published by Tate Publishing & Enterprises, LLC
127 E. Trade Center Terrace | Mustang, Oklahoma 73064 USA
1.888.361.9473 | www.tatepublishing.com

Tate Publishing is committed to excellence in the publishing industry. The company reflects the philosophy established by the founders, based on Psalm 68:11,
"The Lord gave the word and great was the company of those who published it."

Book design copyright © 2012 by Tate Publishing, LLC. All rights reserved.
Cover design by Errol Villamante
Interior design by Jan Sunday Quilaquil

Published in the United States of America

ISBN: 978-1-62024-457-9
1. Fiction / Religious
2. Fiction / Family Life
12.07.13

Foreword

Gary Hamer has written a book I could not put down. From start to finish, page after page, I wanted to find out more about Nykloneci's rise to greatness.

This is a story of good versus evil, the supple hold the dark forces have on day-to-day lives, and how they influence the choices we make.

During Nykloneci's childhood we learn about him living with a father that associated himself with evil and his mother trying to set him on the path to good.

In his somewhat typical teenage years, he rebels, sometimes to excess while his father turns to good and takes an oath to follow the ultimate ruler of the land. In adulthood Nykloneci, now in military service, further continues his self-destructive and deceptive ways until through positive influence by his father arranges for Nykloneci to be trained to serve the ultimate ruler. Training not only involves the hand-to-hand physical combat, but also how to control the elements and how to travel between the eleven dimensions and the perils that are contained within some of them.

Throughout the story we meet good characters who are gracious, faithful, loving and blessed. We also meet evil characters who are manipulative, deceitful, and controlling. Tanas, the rebel leader, and Lustureus will have you cringing; Gammy

will display strength; the Death Messenger will show mercy and compassion; the Crafters will make you think about what next great tool they could create; the Scribe will have you wishing you had half his skills. Overarching all this, King Hertfa, the ultimate ruler of the land, keeps things in check providing faith—and finally, the Singers will have you cheering.
—Stephan Sidorenko

Acknowledgments

I wish to thank Dr. Richard Tate, founder of Tate Publishing and Enterprises, for his help and support of my work. I also wish to thank Mark McDevitt for his help and gracious ability to guide and instruct me in the issues that arise. I would also like to thank my copy editor, Amber Fulton, and my developmental editor, Jessica Browning, for their help and encouragement with the complete process of bringing this book to you, the reader. I also want to thank the entire staff of Tate Publishing and Enterprises for their help and assistance during each step of the process of being willing to help in every way possible. As always I want to thank Irene Sidorenko for her support and help in all of my books, she truly is a wonderful help and encouragement to me.

The Main Characters

Nykloneci—the boy who decides to serve King Hertfa at a young age and the inspiration for this whole series of books.

King Hertfa—the ruler of the empire and the one who maintains balance and leads his people to fight against the tyranny of the dark lords who surround his empire.

Susthris—son of King Hertfa, works to maintain the empire with his father. Susthris has his own belief system, and he supports his father in most areas of life and leadership of his empire. Susthris is a thinker who studies all that has been established to see if any new ways are needed to maintain the empire.

Scribe—a six-armed individual who is in charge of the library of the king and keeps all the records and the books updated for the king about all of his subjects who are worthy to have books written about them as they serve King Hertfa. Scribe holds the key to the empire and can bring it all to an end if he chooses to do so.

Gammy—a mighty warrior and a member of the Royal Guard who serves King Hertfa. Gammy is the one that even his fellow warriors fear because he was nicknamed "the destroyer." He fights to preserve the empire and lives up to his nickname in every battle.

THE BEGINNINGS OF NYKLONECI

Herbance—father of Nykloneci, he served the dark lord Lustureus for many years before breaking free from him and serving King Hertfa. Over many years he attained the position of elder of the king and works to preserve and further the empire of the king with his council and service to the king.

Lucy—mother of Nykloneci, she worked to protect him from his father when he was young. She always saw the best in Nykloneci and worked to help him in every way possible, as every mother would.

Lustureus—a dark lord who constantly battles against the king and tries to take his servants away from him and hold them in bondage. He held Herbance in his service for many years before he broke free from him to serve King Hertfa.

Tanas—a dark lord doing all he can to try to remove the king from his position of authority. Tanas plots and schemes to try everything he can to find a way to get back at King Hertfa ever since he left his service to rule his own life and the lives of anyone he can get to follow him.

Razielle—Death Messenger of the king. He is the one who collects those who are ready to die and takes them to the king. His work is a labor of showing kindness and love towards those who are ready to pass from life and he is often feared and deemed to be evil by the servants of the king because of the service which he provides for King Hertfa. Razielle is the servant of King Hertfa who everyone wants to avoid at all costs and when he does come to check on someone the air turns cold and he can show his glowing red eyes to the people as he passes by.

Table of Contents

Prologue	viii
The Beginnings of Nykloneci	1
The Story Begins	2
The Control of the Dark Lords	16
King Hertfa and His Royal Guard	22
Tanas Leads the Rebellion	27
The Singers of the King	35
The Choice of Herbance	39
Nykloneci's Early Years	48
The Growth of Imagination	62
The Course in Life Changes	67
From the Village to the City	81
The Next Problem Area of Life	85
Service to the King	97
Learning from the Elder	100
Learning to Control the Storms	108
The Warrior Training Begins	115
The Eleven Dimensional Realms	127
The Portal Knowledge	145
The Secrets of the King	152
The Crafters of the King	166
The King's Son	179
The Death Messenger	192
Afterword	209

PROLOGUE

After becoming a Barnes and Noble bestselling author with my second published work, *The Greatest Lie Ever Told*, I determined that it was time for me to use my imagination and create a character that we can all relate to in life. Nykloneci is the child in all of us that aspires to greatness in life without any real plan or understanding of goals and purpose.

We all seem to want to think that we can become someone great and outstanding in life; sadly few ever accomplish or achieve this. But we all have this thought and desire to become more than we ever think we can become. This is the story of Nykloneci. He truly desired to be someone of greatness in his life, and when he got his chance, he grabbed hold of it with a vigor and gusto that everyone can appreciate and admire. We all have a closet full of things that we hope never get out and confront us in life, but as we all know there are times when the door to the closet gets flung open and out comes our worst fear. Learning how to deal with our own personal fears is what allows us to overcome the issues of life. Many times we are brought into the place of fear by things that we truly don't understand. This does not diminish the fear or make it any less real.

Nykloneci had many areas of fear in his life, some were the product of his own doing and others were brought into his life by an attachment that he never realized or understood. Even those people who are destined for greatness are at times only destined for a very short period of time. The end result of the greatness that comes into our lives can cause us to flourish, or it can cause us to wither and die on the vine. Enter in, and join me in this pilgrimage that each of us has to endure in life and follow the pathway that was chosen for Nykloneci. The pathway that can lead to greatness or the pathway to destruction, it is all depending on how we learn to handle the things that come into our lives.

The Beginnings of Nykloneci

This story begins as many do with the ideal of what it takes for somebody to become great in their life. There was a young man who was born in humble circumstances and his upbringing was something out of the ordinary. The basis of this story is how this young man was sanctioned to become someone great for the king. This young man had no aspirations to become anything substantial in his life even though he was a dreamer. This story will chronicle the rise to fame and glory by one Nykloneci and it will document his rise to greatness for the king. This novel will take you along the pathway of his life and allow you to follow his exploits leading up to becoming the general who was in control of all of King Hertfa's army.

The Story Begins

This is a whimsical tale of someone who rose to greatness and how he was able to accomplish this great undertaking in his life. We must begin, as all begin, with all of the information which is needed before his birth and growing up in a small village. This child was born under the most ordinary of circumstances from all outward appearances which anyone could discern without the knowledge of his father's situation and his life was an open book in that he had no great aspirations of greatness.

    Lucy was determined that her life would take a normal route and she would marry her long-time boyfriend of many years. Stanley was her love and he had maintained a relationship with her for many years. Stanley had great dreams and ideals about his life and the life of Lucy and he had plans that they would marry and live happily for many years. Lucy thought things were set in motion for her and that she would lead a normal and uneventful life. Her plan was to marry Stanley and have a house full of children to carry on the name and the legacy of Stanley. The only part that she was not happy about was the decision that Stanley would set her up to operate a fish shop that sold fish to the public in a large southern city. This was one aspect of her life that she truly did not relish or think would be a wonderful experience. Lucy had imagined her life would be filled with taking care of the children. When

THE BEGINNINGS OF NYKLONECI

Stanley mentioned his plans for her this caused her to think about life with him differently. Lucy detested fish in any fashion and to think she would have to handle and deal with fish on a daily basis caused her to reevaluate her life with Stanley. This changed her thoughts about her life in a way which was more than she could bear. Lucy realized Stanley had many ideas about their life together which he had not shared with her. It was at this point of understanding many things had not been discussed and evaluated which began to help her to realize life with Stanley might be something other than she thought. The fact he had not told her about his plans for their long term commitment seemed to create doubts in her mind about him. If he had not shared this part of their future with her until now what else did he have in mind which she knew nothing about? But she knew that over time she could change his mind about this, and it would not come to pass like he planned. Lucy had no understanding that her life was set for a course of anything but normal, and that once things were set in place, her life would never be the same again.

Herbance was arranged to date Lucy's younger sister and start a relationship with her but when they met he realized she was too young and immature for him. Herbance was looking for someone to share his life with who could understand his dreams and desires and he knew immediately this girl was not for him. She was more concerned about what she wanted in life than to have any ability to try to think of something other than herself and her own personal desires. Herbance decided that her older sister Lucy would be a perfect wife for him. The problem with all of this was that Herbance was into a very dramatic source of power that was not positive in any way. He was living his life as a shadow of what he could be because he had turned away from serving King Hertfa many years ago. Lucy had no idea what course her life would eventually take, and once Herbance decided that she was to become his wife, nothing that was said or done was able to change his decision.

It was his way that once Herbance set his mind on something it usually came to pass. He was not able to do this by his own strength or power, but by a power that he had accepted and adopted into his life. Lucy had no idea what he was doing with regard to his service at the time they met. She only knew that there was something interesting and different about him. Herbance was not like any of the other men who Lucy knew—he had a confidence about him and a way of presenting himself that was a natural attractant. The fact about Herbance was that he seemed to be a shy and backward boy, but somehow she knew that he was deep. She did not understand or grasp how and why he was so different.

Lucy's mother, Mayon, tried to warn her that something was terribly wrong with Herbance, but as with most children, she ignored her mother's advice. The concerns of her mother were born of her own life and the mistakes that she had made. Lucy's mother was in bondage at that time, but her bondage was self-imposed, as was Herbance's. Mayon had decided that she would go her own way in life and determine her own destiny.

When Mayon made this choice, she was at a low place in her life and the dark lord Saltro came to her. Saltro was willing to show her what her life could be, if she would accept his help and guidance. Without hesitation, she, too, had turned from serving King Hertfa and had accepted her place as a servant of a dark lord. When people do this, they are able to acknowledge this trait in others. So Lucy's mother realized that there was something terribly wrong with Herbance, but she was not able to determine exactly what it was. Mayon tried to talk to Lucy many times about how something just did not fit with Herbance, but Lucy was not able to grasp or understand what her mother meant.

When people fall under the control of others, it is often hard for them to grasp what is happening to them, and when someone brings this to their attention, they are often unable to understand. Lucy decided her mother was just jealous of her and that Herbance had come into her life after Stanley had gone off to the big city to learn a trade for his future. Stanley had determined that he wanted a better life for Lucy and himself, so his desire was to advance and become someone through his learning a trade. The problem came into play that while Stanley was away in the big city, he found his new freedoms were more than he could handle. He began to notice the other women in the city, and he became infatuated with some of them and his love for Lucy had begun to wane and grow cold.

This new freedom which he experienced was something that he had never had before. His mother, Trista, was always controlling him and keeping him in check while he lived at home. She was always comparing him to his father Farndo and telling him that he was not going to follow the same pathway in life as his father. Farndo was not a good husband to Trista, nor a good father to his children. He spent too much time drinking his life away and throwing his meager earnings into new schemes to become rich. He was a dreamer, and with a wife and three children, he needed to be firmly grounded and working to support his family. But alas, he was busy with his schemes and his drinking, and he did not have the time or energy to devote to working. Trista had to help by going to work and making up the difference in what Farndo was unable to provide for the family.

This was the life of Stanley—up to this point—before he decided to leave for the big city and learn a trade, he was always being told what to do and how to do it by Trista. He was constantly under her control and guidance, and this made him feel like he would never have a life of his own. Stanley felt like his life was lived in the shadow of his father and in the light of his mother. His father was always busy with a new scheme to come up with money to support the family without working for it. Trista was always there watching his every move and telling him that he would not become like his father if she had anything to do with his life.

Stanley knew that he would not be like his father because he had ambition. But without his mother's constant watchful eye upon him in the city, he was able to begin to sample what other women had to offer. Stanley loved that his mother was not putting him under her thumb like she did at home, and this was a new adventure for him. He did not realize that his time away was hurting his relationship with Lucy. He did not even notice that many times when he came home from the city, he would often neglect to even go see her. He was too busy with his dreams and plans for the future; he was trying to make a good life for himself and Lucy and besides, what he did in the big city would never come home to roost in his life.

Stanley decided that he would never tell Lucy what he experienced in the city and he would often forget to go see her because he was so busy thinking about the next thing he needed to do to set his life in order. Stanley had great plans for his life and he knew that he would become someone great, but little did he know that his plans would all come to a slow and gradual end. Stanley did not grasp or understand that he had things going well in his life. Once he came to understand that his plans were all tied together with his relationship with Lucy, he made some long-term plans that never came to pass. This set his life on a course for disappointment and discouragement that he would never have imagined for himself, but alas life changes and not always for what we want to think we need.

Stanley was confident that the things he did while he was away in the big city were far enough away that Lucy would never find out and that would be a very good thing for him. Stanley was confident that all he was doing to prepare for his future life with Lucy would benefit them both. He did not grasp that there was even the hint of a problem on the horizon of his life. He just thought that he was finally out from under his mother's thumb and it felt so wonderful to have freedom that he never had at home.

By the time he realized that problems had crept in on his plans, Herbance had already made his presence known, and this caused great problems and confusion for Stanley. Stanley could not understand why someone would come and disrupt his plans and goals in life. He did not think this would be much of a problem because he knew that Lucy was faithful to him no matter what he did behind her back. After all, what she did not know could not hurt her, and he had no intention of telling her what was going on in his life at the time he was away in the big city to learn his trade. Stanley realized his mistake of telling Lucy they needed to see other people even though he was the one who had suggested that this needed to happen for them to be happy later in life.

The truth of this whole situation was the last time Stanley was home from the city, he made a decision that both he and Lucy should date other people so they would be better prepared for life as a couple. He had no clue that this was the beginning of the end for his plans. His own desire to invest some time with the women in the city was clouding his mind and causing him to push Lucy away. He was using his newfound freedom to expand his experiences, and he started to feel guilty with what he was doing while he was away from home. He thought that if he pushed Lucy to date other men, this would lessen his guilt and allow him to continue on with his plans. What he did not realize was that with each new woman he spent time with; it lessened his desire for Lucy.

While he was away enjoying his new life in the big city, Lucy was beginning to feel like something dramatic had changed between them. When he came home she would often wait for him to come to see her, and over time he did this less and less. She would find out that he was home, and when he did not show up to see her, she knew that things were changing. She began to have dreams of what he was doing during his training in the city, and she was able to feel how distant he was becoming to her.

That last visit when he said that they needed to begin dating other people so their bond could become stronger only showed her that things would never be the same again between them. She began to feel like her life was not going to be what she had planned and his insistence that they begin to spend time apart for a while only pushed her farther away from him. Stanley was being used by a dark lord to prepare a way for Lucy and Herbance to come together so that Nykloneci would be born into the world. Little did anyone grasp or real-

THE BEGINNINGS OF NYKLONECI

ize that Lustureus was working behind the scenes and doing what was necessary to break the bond that Lucy and Stanley had built together.

After the time that Lucy and Herbance began dating, Stanley came home from his training in the big city and begged Lucy to come back to him. They talked, and it was decided that she would have to tell Herbance that it was over between them, and she was ready for Stanley to come back into her life. Her mother Mayon even got involved and tried her best to explain the plans that Stanley had made would be best for her, and she needed to realize that Herbance was not part of this plan. Mayon even invoked her dark lord Saltro to try to stop Herbance from having access to her daughter Lucy.

Saltro was an ancient dark lord with a unique ability to appear as a large white beast with fangs and claws. When Saltro made this transformation, he would stand about ten feet tall and have a reach of about eight feet with his claws. Saltro would use this effect whenever he wanted to produce fear in the people that he wanted to scare into submission. The fact that he had been in control of Mayon was paramount because he had also been in control of her mother, Ealsa. Saltro had learned well what it took to maintain control of this family, and he was always on the prowl for any new family that he could gain control over and bring into his circle of followers. Saltro was watching to see which one of Mayon's children would be open for his guidance and control. He knew that once someone was identified as being open to him, he would have someone else to help in life and gain control over them until they served him the way he desired.

Saltro made his proposal of help and protection by allowing the people who followed him to think that they could control him and chain him up in their storage spaces. Saltro would provide the chains and pretend to be bound by the people that he wanted to be his. This ploy made it possible for him to maintain control over them while they thought that they were the ones in control of him. This proposition allowed the people to feel safe and that they were protected because this beast would allow them to chain him and control him. What the people did not realize was that once they thought Saltro was safely bound and locked away, he would leave and search for new followers. This proved to be a dramatic mistake because Mayon did not realize that Lustureus was more powerful than Saltro and this created quite a problem for her.

The time came when Mayon requested Saltro to go and cause problems and bring harm to Herbance. Saltro decided that he would appear as this great white beast and bring fear to Herbance. Saltro waited until he felt like Herbance was vulnerable, and then he struck. He appeared without warning on the roadway in front of Herbance's carriage and attempted to swipe it with his claws and force it off the road. Herbance was able to guide his carriage off the roadway and avoid most of the blow that Saltro was trying to inflict. Saltro thought this would be an adequate warning to Herbance to show him that he was in control and that he should listen to Mayon and follow her desires. When Herbance brought Lucy back home after this event took place, Mayon was feeling like she had gained the upper hand in the situation and that things were now under the control of Saltro. She listened as Herbance explained to her that this was an event that would only cause many problems for her and her dark lord. Herbance told Mayon that he would have to involve Lustureus in this issue and once this happened, she would know the power of his dark lord.

When the confrontation between Saltro and Lustureus was over, Saltro was bloodied and bruised from the battle which ensued between them and he refused to interfere from this point on. Mayon was distressed once she realized that she was dealing with something that had more power than her own dark lord and this brought fear to her. She had always felt like Saltro was able to defend her and her family, and now she realized that her faith in him was misplaced. Mayon began to question why she had fallen under the control of Saltro, now that he was shown to be inferior in his abilities to protect and help. Mayon began to think that it might be time for her to withdraw from her service to Saltro and find another dark lord who was stronger and able to help her. Saltro had a firm grip on Mayon's life, and he would remain in control of her and keep her as his servant—there was no way that he would allow her to leave him. Mayon had willingly come to him and asked his help and now he was not going to break this bond and allow her to leave his service.

This only led to Mayon's continued discussions with Lucy about Herbance and why she should get away from him and move on with her life. She tried at every turn to get Lucy to go back to Stanley, but it was all to no avail. This constant barrage of Mayon only caused Lucy to withdraw from her mother, and she had never done this before. Mayon realized that she was driving her daughter away but only after it was too late to mend the differences.

Lucy was beginning to think for herself and this was a good thing. This was the beginning of Lucy being able to think for herself and make her own decisions. Lucy had never done this before in her life. Her mother was always there to give her council and help her decide what to do, but now this was all changing. Lucy began to question all the things which Mayon had decided for her, and she saw with a new clarity that her life was her own. This caused Mayon to begin to fear Herbance and Lustureus more than she had before.

Mayon's daughter Lucy was finally seeing life through her own eyes and not being swayed by anyone else now. Lucy had become her own person and knew that she was now in charge of her own destiny. This was the turning point for Lucy; she now knew that no matter what life threw her way she was able to stand firm and make her own decisions. This was the beginning of her understanding that life is only what you make of it, and she was determined that her life would be her own from now on.

Lucy took the time to look at her life in a fresh and wonderful way—she now realized that the control of Mayon was broken off of her life and she was now able to live life for herself. This freeing and liberating moment changed Lucy, and she was determined that nothing and nobody would ever force her into following something that she did not support wholeheartedly. Lucy had become her own person and nothing would change this in her life again.

It was at this time of decision in her life that Lucy steeled herself and broke the power of her mother Mayon off of her life. She had no way of knowing at the time that her stand against her mother was also a stand against Saltro. Saltro had become such a dominate force in the life of Mayon that he was one with her in every way possible. When Lucy stood against Mayon, she was also standing against Saltro.

This decision was the turning point, and it helped Lucy to understand that no matter what came in life, she would be a force to be reckoned with. She would stand firm in her own beliefs and desires from this day forward. This time of decision became a marker in her life and one that she would look back to many times as the years passed. She was no longer under the control of Mayon or Saltro, and with this servitude broken off of her life she would not be subjected to Lustureus through her future husband Herbance.

Lucy had gained her independence from the need to have anyone tell her what to do or when to do it. From this point forward in her life, she would be her own person and would follow the path that King Hertfa had set for her. With this one time of decision where Lucy truly made her own choice, she set the pathway for her life and nothing would ever stop her again. Lucy was her own person now, and nothing could change this fact for her. Lucy had finally stepped out of the shadow of her mother Mayon, and now she was going to live her own life her own way. Lucy decided for herself to follow her pathway in life and make her own choices and she chose to marry Herbance.

She had married Herbance because of his persistence. She thought her pathway in life was settled and decided until Herbance entered her life and swept her off her feet in a very peculiar and unusual way. Herbance had entered her life by accident, or so she thought, because he was arranged to date her younger sister. Lucy had made her own choice in this matter and she decided to see if Herbance could provide for her in the way she wanted. Herbance had no ideas of her working in a fish shop and this helped to sway her ideas and form her opinions. In spite of the constant barrage of her mother

Mayon to return to Stanley Lucy had decided to follow the course in life which now had Herbance in it.

With this decision made, Lucy and Herbance were married and settled in a small village where they could start their lives together without the interference of Lucy's mother. The setting was ideal for them both and as long as Lucy could feel like she was loved it was all she needed for now. Within a couple of years together it was time for the new baby to be born. Lucy worried about the child and knew that somehow he would be everything she wanted him to be but she also knew it was imperative that she watch over him carefully. The time came for the baby to be born and he was healthy and beautiful to Lucy. Nothing could keep her from admitting she had made the right choice now with this new life she had delivered into the world. Nykloneci was brought into the world, and Lucy was sure this was her destiny to raise and nurture this child.

Nykloneci was an ordinary child with the same hopes and dreams as most children. He wanted to be someone special but had no driving force to direct his life and create for him any monumental circumstances. Lucy wondered when Nykloneci was born if he would change the world in some special way but as with most mothers she accepted him for what he was.

Nykloneci was a healthy child and was born in a circumstance that was anything but a normal situation in life. His father was in the service of a dark lord who controlled his life and this caused great fear to enter Nykloneci's life from an early age. Nykloneci's mother, Lucy was a normal person without any hindrances that would not allow her to give full attention to her child. She was a jolly woman who made the best of life and did what was necessary to bring about what

THE BEGINNINGS OF NYKLONECI

she wanted in life. Lucy was a worker but only in the things of keeping her hands busy and her watchful eye on Nykloneci. She knew that one day her son would make her proud and bring her true happiness, but only if she could manage to keep him away from the darkness of her husband Herbance.

Lucy understood that things were going on with Herbance that were not normal or comforting to her. Because of her knowledge about what Herbance was doing and her desire to keep Nykloneci safe, she agreed to work around the home and stay close to her son and guard his life. She realized and understood that Herbance never wanted children, so in the back of her mind she often wondered what might happen if she let things go in the natural progression in life. This thought worried her, so she determined that she would always keep a watchful eye on Nykloneci and make sure that nothing untoward happened to him. In her heart, she knew that Herbance was a servant of evil and she wanted to be sure that Nykloneci was given a chance to avoid this if at all possible in his life.

Lucy determined she was the one who would support and encourage Nykloneci throughout his life and she would always be there for him. She decided he would be given the chance to live his life free from the anguish and slavery which his father had in his life. Lucy was the one who stood in the way of anything that could come to Nykloneci to harm him or to cause him suffering. After his birth and start to life, Lucy was his friend and protector and the one who believed in him no matter what happened.

The Control of the Dark Lords

The unknown part of the equation was that Nykloneci's father, Herbance, was the servant of a dark lord. This dark lord was Lustureus, and he was in direct rebellion against King Hertfa. He was the one who was growing in power and authority, and he would do anything that was possible to maintain control over the people who fell under his control. The people had to willingly submit to him and then he was a ruthless taskmaster to them. Lustureus offered freedom to anyone who was under the control of King Hertfa, but the freedom that he offered was only a smokescreen to his true aspirations.

In truth, Lustureus was determined to take as many of the king's subjects and turn them against him as he possibly could. He was a master of waiting for the right moment to present his services to anyone who was not happy with the king. Lustureus knew from his many years that if he waited for the right moment, and presented his case, he would gather many followers who had been faithful to King Hertfa and turn them to serving him. His desire was to gather as many loyal subjects to himself and then he would gain the power and following needed to change the world and bring King Hertfa pain and suffering.

Lustureus would show up with visions of grandeur, and he would seduce the people into believing he could offer them something that the king could not offer to them. The truth was Lustureus was only looking to gain a following that would commit to him and do his bidding without any kind of help or support from him. This was his way of controlling and manipulating the people who fell into his clutches and this is what made him so dangerous. His approach was to seek out those who were in need of serious and oftentimes immediate help, and he would gain their trust by telling them that he could help. After the seeds of his evil were planted in the lives of the people, it was only a matter of time before they came completely under his control and would serve him completely.

The dark lord Lustureus was working to build himself an empire of his own choosing. He would willingly accept anyone who had a grievance with the king. Lustureus was keen on finding as many loyal subjects as he could to help him in his quest to become equal with King Hertfa. Lustureus was growing in power and had a following which would soon be able to rival the king. He knew that when his time came, he would have a good chance of removing King Hertfa from power and replace him with his own wicked desires. All it took was for more people to follow him and believe his lies and allow him to attach to their lives and place them in servitude for their existence in life. Lustureus knew that it was only a matter of time and then he would be able to overthrow King Hertfa. All it took was waiting for the proper time and more followers would come to him and then the time would come for him to strike against the king.

The way that the dark lords held those who came to serve them in captivity was through the use of their minds. Once someone came to serve any of the dark lords, their best and initial way to control them was for the dark lords to give their own memories to those who came to serve. The memories of the dark lords were a combination of what they had accomplished and the pain and suffering they had inflicted on those who came before to serve them. Once someone decided to serve the dark lords, the memories of the dark lords came to them and they became their own personal memories. The dark lords were able to interject these memories into the minds of the people and this is what caused them to continue their service to them. The memories became real to each person in the service of the dark lords. The memories were personalized in a way that each person believed they had committed these atrocities. Unspeakable times of torture and murder and horrible things being done to innocent people. This was the hold the dark lords were expert at maintaining—once they got your allegiance to serve them, they would place their memories within your mind. They interacted in your mind in such a way that you became the one who did all the things they brought to your memory. It was not someone else who was doing these things, it was you and you alone doing all that happened.

This power to control the mind is what allowed the dark lords to maintain their hold and control of those who started serving them. The memories were so vivid and real, each person thought they had committed what they remembered. But, alas, it was only the memories of the dark lords which were firmly implanted into the minds of their servants. This helped them to maintain the control that they needed to continue their hold on their lives. This is the secret of the dark lords; they implant what they want you to believe. And then they constantly remind you of what you did, nothing that you actually were involved with, but something which they made you believe you did.

THE BEGINNINGS OF NYKLONECI

This is truly the ultimate in mind control and mind games. But since they had done this so many times to so many of their faithful followers which they had gained, it is easy for them to continue this activity to maintain control. The dark lords are all masters at this process and it is essentially the same for them all. All they need to do is implant their memories and then remind those in their service of what they have done. This keeps them under their control and power for as long as they stay in this position in life.

The mind is established as a place for them to keep you in check by giving their memories to each person. They begin to do the physical things that bring pain and suffering. Many times when Herbance was under the control of Lustureus, he would feel the pain and see the effects of what he was subjected to in his life. The constant shame and feelings of being pure evil through the memories implanted in his mind. Herbance lived a tortured and horrible life of the guilt of things he did not commit but believed he had premeditated and carried out.

Many times Lustureus would come and place large fish hooks in his back and legs from behind and then hang him on chains that would place all of his weight on the fish hooks. This practice brought excruciating pain to Herbance, and after these sessions were over, he would have large open sores where the hooks had been inserted into his flesh. Terrible pain was often inflicted upon the most faithful servants of the dark lords as a way to keep them following the pathway to destruction.

Most people never realized that they had any other choice but to continue to serve their dark masters. Once the mind control was established the physical suffering was always to follow. Many times the dark lords would invite other dark lords to come and bring pain to their servants. This is the dramatic and devastating part of service to darkness. One dark lord is never satisfied with inflicting all that they can upon their followers. They constantly invite other dark lords to inflict punishment and pain, different from what they are able to do, so that their power can be maintained and their followers forced to comply.

After the mind control and physical pain has been established, the final step is undertaken and the spiritual aspect is attacked until it is broken down and put in submission. The spirit is left for last in case something happens that one of the other parts cannot be implemented. In the few cases where this happened, the spirit was never broken into by the dark lords, and over time they relinquished control on their own until they could find other dark lords to help them break down the defenses of their quarry.

The dark lords are in no hurry, they have the element of time on their side. With enough time and the right application, they are able to break down anyone who refuses to submit to them. Once the spiritual aspect of the servant is effectively broken down, the dark lords close in for the kill and inflict their will on their followers with ruthless and unrelenting terror. Many times once this stage is entered, the servant begs for death to come and take them. Their pleas go unanswered because they are no longer free to ask for this on their own. They have a new master in the dark lords whom they serve, and the will of the dark lords enters into the equation from this point. Servitude and pain are awaiting all of those people who fall within the grasp of the dark lords, and even when they pray and ask for death, it is withheld from them.

Those under the control of the dark lords are never free to ask for anything for themselves again in life. Everything must be in agreement to what the dark lords' desire and nothing will come to their servants without their consent and approval. All the servants of the dark lords lose themselves once they allow the dark lords total access to them in every way. This is the power of the dark lords, deception and interjection of their own thoughts and memories is what keeps the servants faithful. The servants honestly accept and believe that they have done what their memories tell them. They never question if they did what they saw in their minds, they only accept what they believe to have happened and this is what keeps them in the service of the dark lords.

King Hertfa and His Royal Guard

King Hertfa is the ultimate ruler of the land, but he had some in his kingdom who were not loyal to him or willing to serve him any longer. This was the basis for the dark lords who were rising from their place to try to become equal to the king. Many of these dark lords had risen, and they were doing all they could to turn the loyal subjects of the king away from their service to him. They promised freedom to any who would follow them and serve their cause. This brought many to fall away from following the king and set their minds and energy to help advance the various dark lords that were leading the rebellions which had started in the land of the king.

The king was gracious and willing to accept anyone who wished to follow him faithfully, and many who had accepted to follow and serve him saw the opportunity that the dark lords offered. It was a time of great revolt and rebellion throughout the land of the king. The dark lords were able to establish their followers and this allowed those faithful to the king to diminish at times. The king knew this rebellion was being led against him by the dark lords. King Hertfa stood by and allowed this to happen to see the true followers that he had who would remain faithful to him and follow his leading. The king knew that many would leave his service to follow the dark lords, but he also knew that this time of great rebellion would come.

The king had many people who remained faithful to him and this was his place of authority in the land. The king provided protection and peace to those who remained faithful and stayed with him through this time of the great falling away. The king knew that many would refuse to stay with his purpose and follow his leading. But he allowed those who left to go because it was their personal decision, and he allowed them to make this choice. King Hertfa allowed his servants the free will to decide if they would continue in his service or go over to the dark lords and serve them.

King Hertfa has been in control for as long as anyone could remember. His time seemed to go on and on, and everyone knew that he had been king for a long time. Yet, even with this nobody questioned his ability or authority to be king. He had the appearance of someone who had survived a long time, but when the people saw him coming, they always bowed in reverence to him.

It had been so long since anyone truly took the time to look at him that most could no longer describe how he looked. It had become such a tradition to bow when he came by, that nobody ever stood and looked at him. This fed the legend that King Hertfa was an immortal and that he had always been king and would always be king. Nobody could ever remember anyone else being king besides King Hertfa. When a search was done to find out who was king before King Hertfa, no mention was ever given of any other king in any of the records of the land. This was such an interesting and unusual outcome, but whenever it was mentioned, people would always say that King Hertfa was always the king and would always be the king. King Hertfa placed tremendous influence in the lives of all of his subjects. The king was willing to supply what they needed if they took an oath to serve him faithfully. Once anyone had done this, they came under his protection and his blessings. King Hertfa was a gracious and loving king; he would travel around throughout his realm and spend time with the people who were loyal to him.

When King Hertfa traveled, he was always accompanied by his royal guard. These were the highest elite guard of the king and only those who had served him faithfully for many years were given the opportunity to join in their ranks. The king insisted that there only be eighteen in this company and he was confident that no more were needed to protect him and accompany him when he went on his travels. King Hertfa had this much confidence in his royal guard and they traveled with him throughout his realm.

When King Hertfa traveled to visit the people, he would always prepare a time of allowing them to come to him so he could hear their grievances. He was a fair and just king, and wherever he went to see the people, he would always set aside time to listen to them and answer their questions. The royal guard was always with him, and many times it was only a portion of them that accompanied him in these travels. At times, the king would leave some of his royal guard to keep watch on the throne room and maintain it so that it could not be infiltrated by his enemies. These mighty warriors had proven themselves in battles for the king. King Hertfa knew they would be faithful to him as long as he maintained his power over his kingdom. King Hertfa knew that all of the dark lords would gladly take control of his throne room when he went to travel the land. He also knew they could access his throne room because they had the knowledge of how to go to this place and they could take control of it if he did not leave some of the royal guard to maintain it in his absence.

Many dark lords had arisen over the years to try to take part of the territory and the faithful servants away from King Hertfa. But most times when this happened, it only took a visit from the king to show his power and authority, and the dark lords fled. When this happened, it left the people who had attempted to follow the dark lords to suffer the wrath of the king, and it was harsh treatment for them at times. The king knew that he had to show his authority to maintain his following of the people who were faithful to him. When the king traveled throughout his land many times the land would react to his coming. Most times when King Hertfa came to visit the land, it would quiver and shake. This became the way that most of his loyal servants would know when he was coming to their area. The ground would shake and volcanoes would erupt at his approach and at times, the mountains would split open and fall apart. This led the people to think the king had intense and absolute power over their land. This control over the land brought fear to most of the people because some kind of reaction was always evidenced any time the king passed through to visit. What the people did not understand or realize was when the king and his royal guard would come to their territory, the power that they wielded caused this kind of reaction. This happened because of who they were and what they could do with this seemingly unlimited power which they possessed.

During these travels of the king, the dark lords were made aware of his coming by what happened to the land. They would have time to leave and evacuate their places before he came to them directly. The king usually avoided the dark lords totally and would be sure to stay clear of them. Since the land would react to his approach, it was a built-in alarm for the dark lords to know when they needed to evacuate their places of power. Once the king approached them, they would have to leave because of the power which came with the king and the royal guard. No dark lord was able to stay and maintain what they had established once the king decided to come to their area and visit the people.

Tanas Leads the Rebellion

The dark lords had learned this after the first and most powerful one, called Tanas, tried to stand up to the king. Tanas determined that he would stay and maintain his place of power and authority while King Hertfa was visiting the people in his area. The dark lord Tanas drew up his followers and tried to battle the king and his elite royal guard to stop them and overpower them so that he could establish his place for all time. Once he had determined he would be able to stand against the king with his followers, he laid a trap which he knew the king would fall into. The king was gracious and compassionate to his followers, and the dark lord had captured several of those people who were loyal to the king. Tanas had placed them within a small clearing that was surrounded by mountains for the king to see as he traveled through this area.

Tanas knew the king would have compassion on his followers, and he would rush in to save them and free them from their bonds. Tanas knew that once this happened, he would be able to force the king and his elite guard into the clearing. They would be walled in and have to fight him from a distinct disadvantage. Tanas knew the only way to get to the people he had captured was for the king and his royal guard to move through a mountain pass. Once the king and the royal guard got through the pass into the clearing, the trap would close on the king and he would have to fight his way out. The plan was made by Tanas and the king came to this area and when he saw the people who were faithful to him in this clearing, he charged straight to them and his royal guard followed.

Tanas had hidden his troops along the tree line that led to the clearing, and he gave them specific instructions to allow the king and his royal guard to pass them and enter into the box canyon. Tanas knew that after this action was taken the king and his royal guard would be trapped and have to fight their way out. The plan would have worked perfectly if Tanas was up against an ordinary group of warriors. They would have been trapped and would have met their doom at his hand. But Tanas forgot that the king had power which was unrivaled in the land. The plan of Tanas would have succeeded if he was fighting against normal adversaries, but this was King Hertfa and his royal guard.

Tanas had used this plan to battle the people who had been loyal to King Hertfa before and it had worked on them. What Tanas did not realize was the power of the king and his elite warriors was unrivaled in all the land. Once they entered into the box canyon and the clearing which Tanas had determined would be their final resting place, he knew that he had won. King Hertfa and the royal guard freed the captives and then turned to face Tanas and his warriors.

Tanas had an intimate knowledge of King Hertfa because he had served the king for many years as his loyal subject. This insight was his downfall because Tanas had been expelled from the palace of the king because he was always the one who was trying to become equal with the king. It was amazing that someone whom the king had shown his favor and love to would try to overthrow his benefactor and take his place. King

Hertfa knew that the heart of Tanas was filled with an evil desire to remove him from his place as king. King Hertfa also knew that Tanas' desire was to humiliate him and destroy him if he could. When his plan was revealed to King Hertfa, he had no choice but to banish Tanas and remove him from his palace. Tanas vowed that one day he would get his revenge on the king. Tanas knew when he had his chance, he would have to move swiftly and strike the king down with all the strength that he could muster.

This time of service to the king had been a monumental time for Tanas. King Hertfa did not withhold any good thing from him. Tanas had the best standing with the king and would go into his presence every day. Tanas would bask in the glory of the king until his heart turned toward evil and he saw himself on the throne of King Hertfa. Tanas thought he knew all which the king possessed, and that with his carefully laid plan, he would be able to remove the king and take his place. Tanas even believed that the royal guard would follow him and be faithful to him as they had been to King Hertfa. This false sense came to Tanas because he had served the king as his chief servant and was at his beck and call whenever he needed something.

Tanas had been the servant who stood beside King Hertfa as he had listened to the complaints and the needs of the people who came to see him. Tanas had even handed the king his scrolls and his parchments as he made decisions and had them recorded in his library of records. Tanas grew to hate listening to the complaints of the people who came to King Hertfa. He vowed he would make them all his servants and he would be the evil taskmaster that they could never imagine. Tanas knew that when his time came, he would cause much pain and suffering for all the ones who had seen him standing beside the king. He would bring so much suffering to the people who constantly came to the king seeking his help and assistance. Tanas was going to be a force the people would know and never underestimate. He would replace the king one day and pay them back for all that he felt they owed him. Tanas hated the memory of standing and listening to all the complaints of the people while he was with the king. Because of this, he would bring suffering and pain to all of them for their entire lives.

All of the dark lords had served King Hertfa at one time. This is what made them so dangerous once they turned away from serving the king and going their own way. They all knew the king and understood what he did and why he made the decisions that he made. Since they had all served King Hertfa, the king knew what they were capable of, and he knew when he was close to them. King Hertfa had a built-in sense of who he was dealing with in regard to the dark lords. In the past, he knew each one of them intimately. Part of the issue with the dark lords was that Tanas had corrupted them and told them he was going to be king in the place of King Hertfa. Many of the dark lords thought this would be a very good idea and they threw their lot in with Tanas and left the service of the king. Little did they know that the royal guard knew of their plan and had already informed King Hertfa of their impending defection from his service.

The royal guard of King Hertfa had amazing and unusual talents because they always seemed to know what was coming next for the king. Many times they would act on what they knew before the king was informed because they were so efficient in their service to the king. But anytime something this dramatic took place, they always seemed to know about it before it happened. Once they knew, the king would be informed and involved with whatever came to pass as soon as they could give him the information they had gathered. At times, it was only a report of what had already transpired because they moved with such efficiency and would deal with issues before they had time to inform the king.

The problem with Tanas was that he was a boaster and one who could not keep quiet about what he planned to do. He would make open boasts about his time of being king and he would broadcast his plan to anyone who he thought might be able to help him and benefit his position. This was his downfall—he was arrogant and would state that he would be king for everyone to hear, and this was how the royal guard got information about his activities. The royal guard had even approached Tanas to question him about his motives and intentions. He was so arrogant that he told them plainly he planned to overthrow the king and take his place as master of the land. Tanas also explained that once he became king, he expected the royal guard to follow him and protect him the same way they did for King Hertfa. Nothing could stop Tanas in his boasting and arrogance; he continued to broadcast his plans for all to hear and know about.

The royal guard knew it would only be a matter of time before Tanas would act on his threat, so they approached the king and informed him of this plan. King Hertfa wasted no time in banishing Tanas from his service and his kingdom. Tanas was surprised that the king would be so bold as to banish him. Tanas truly thought the king would relinquish his position and allow him and his followers to take control of the territory. Tanas had become so blinded by his thirst for control and being the king, that he thought it would all fall in place for him without much of a problem. When King Hertfa called him in and explained that he would not relinquish his position, Tanas gathered his forces and decided he would have an outright battle and take control. King Hertfa knew Tanas would react this way, so when he arrived with his forces the king was ready. His mounted troops joined with the people in his service to overcome Tanas and his forces. He was removed from service to the king and banished to a small area of the king's territory where he was to live out his existence.

Whenever King Hertfa had to travel close to this area where Tanas was banished from the king and his palace, Tanas would make every attempt to intercept the king and engage him in battle again. The king knew that he could overthrow and destroy Tanas with his troops and his royal guard. But he felt compassion and mercy toward him because of his many years of service to him. King Hertfa was not able to destroy Tanas and his followers because he still hoped that one day he might come to his senses and realize what he had done.

Many people said King Hertfa was too lenient on Tanas. They wondered why this was allowed to continue for all of the years in which it had gone on. The king would not discuss this matter of Tanas with anyone. When the subject was brought up, King Hertfa would only say he was dealing with Tanas and his group of followers the best way possible. Nobody realized the king knew Tanas intimately, and since he did, he knew that this adversary would always try to overthrow him. But King Hertfa also knew there would be fighting within the ranks of Tanas and his followers. Since King Hertfa knew that this group would never unite fully, he did not see them as a great threat to himself. King Hertfa knew that one day he would confront Tanas and call him to account. But King Hertfa was waiting and hoping that one day Tanas would come to his senses and ask the king for forgiveness.

Tanas had captured several people within the area that King Hertfa was going to be traveling through. It was almost like Tanas thought he knew what the king would do and where he would go. And of course, since the land reacted to the arrival of the king, this may have helped Tanas to figure out where the king was going next. Most times when King Hertfa traveled throughout his territory, the land would react by convulsing and thrashing about as if something had caused it pain or created some type of glimmer in its existence. Many times when the king came to an area, his arrival would create earthquakes, tidal waves, or volcanic eruptions to happen because of his presence. This was not a direct result of what the king commanded; it was just a natural reaction from the physical world to his entering into it. It was almost as if the land knew that the power of the king would create reactions within it. The land had to react to King Hertfa's appearing and coming through it in this way.

The scene was set, and Tanas knew that once the king found out he had captured some of his beloved and loyal subjects, there would be no way the king would allow this to continue. Tanas knew if he could only get the king off guard and make him do something that might tip the balance of the fight in his favor; he might have his chance to do away with King Hertfa.

Tanas thought that this day was the day of his advancement, since he thought he knew what the king would do and rescue those people he had captured. Tanas set his warriors behind the trees to camouflage their position and waited for the king and his troops to see the people and attempt their rescue. He knew that once the king determined it was time to go and save his subjects, he would be ready and waiting to close the trap on the king. Tanas would finally get his chance to destroy King Hertfa and take the royal guard as his own warriors.

King Hertfa and his royal guard advanced on the box canyon that Tanas had determined would give him the advantage which he knew he would need. The king and his troops entered and went to the people and began to set them free when Tanas and his troops entered. The only way out of this canyon was effectively blocked by Tanas and his troops and they began to advance on the king and his troops. Tanas thought that the king was finished and his plan had finally worked after all of these failed attempts.

The Singers of the King

King Hertfa looked up and saw Tanas and his troops were closing in on his royal guard and faithful followers. The king gave the command to go to battle, and his troops drew their swords and grabbed their shields and turned to face Tanas.

Tanas outnumbered the king and his troops ten to one, and he knew that if he failed in this attempt, he would never get another chance like this. Tanas and his troops surrounded the king and started to move in for the kill. It was at this moment King Hertfa raised his sword and called out that it was time to sing. The royal guard stood their ground and waited to see what was coming at the king's command for the singers to approach.

Tanas knew that once the singers began to sing, he and his forces would be powerless to fight. A group of singers came marching through the pass, and they began to sing. When they did, all of Tanas' troops, and even he, began to weep, and they could not fight. The singers were a secret weapon which the king used when fighting against forces of evil. Once the singers started to sing, the evil troops became powerless to fight. The singing was such a harmonious and melodious event that all who heard the singing started to weep. Tanas knew the king had singers, but he was not aware that when King Hertfa traveled throughout the land, he had some of the singers accompany him. Tanas had stood in the presence of the king and listened to the singers for many years. He knew once they began to sing, peace came over all who heard them. He also knew that once the singers began, they would not stop until the king commanded them to finish their singing. Tanas looked on as his troops dropped their weapons and began to sob uncontrollably. King Hertfa knew the memories of these dark lords and their followers would cause them to suffer in ways which nobody could understand. When the singers sang, it brought back the memories of when they were faithful to the king and standing in his presence.

Once the dark lords started remembering where they had come from and what they had become, the singing caused them to stop whatever they were doing and weep and mourn for what they had left. Tanas was defeated and it was all done with only a song, the king knew this was his best defense against the dark lords. King Hertfa had instituted a long time ago that whenever he went out to travel the land of his kingdom, singers would always accompany him. King Hertfa knew if they were ever in such a position as this one, the singers would sing and there would be no need for bloodshed. King Hertfa knew that once they heard the singing, any of the dark lords would be taken back to when they were his faithful servants. The message of the singing always invoked this reaction to anyone who had been in the service of the king. The singing brought the dark lords back to the time when they were faithful servants of the king and weeping was always a part of this process. The dark lords knew they had made a terrible mistake whenever they heard the singing, and they had nothing to do but weep and mourn for what they remembered. The songs of the singers always reminded the dark lords of their time of standing in the presence of the king and being his faithful servants. This process took them back to when they realized what they had and what they had lost in their rebellion to the king.

King Hertfa knew the singing was always a powerful influence on all of the dark lords and those who followed them. There were only a few of the dark lord's followers who had never served the king. When the singing started it never affected those who had never served King Hertfa personally. They saw the effect on the dark lords and their followers, and when this happened, they always dropped their weapons and fled. The ones who had never been in the service of the king could not understand how a song could create such a place of bitter weeping for the dark lords. They only knew that once the singing started, any battle was over immediately.

King Hertfa and his troops freed the people and herded them past Tanas and his troops while the singers were engaged in their song. The king had once again thwarted the plans of Tanas and left him and his troops weeping bitterly in the box canyon. After all the people had been taken out of the canyon, King Hertfa came back and commanded the singers to finish their song. The singers ended the song and marched out of the canyon with the king following them.

Tanas now knew he had no chance of catching the king off guard from that moment forward. Any plan which he could make would always end in failure and he would never get to replace King Hertfa. After the king and his troops left and the singers had ended their song and marched away, Tanas called his troops and dispersed them. He instructed them to go out into the entire territory of the king and find people who had never served the king. He commanded to take them into captivity and instruct them in the ways of war and prepare them for the battle that would come one day in the future.

Tanas knew anyone who had ever served the king would not be able to fight against the king once the singers sang their song. Tanas was determined to raise an army that would not be affected by the singing. Tanas knew when he was able to gain this advantage, one day he would make King Hertfa pay. The followers of Tanas began that day to scour the land and find those who had never served King Hertfa and to take every advantage of them to bring them into his service.

The Choice of Herbance

This is the way it was for Nykloneci's father; he had decided that his life was in a terrible place and he finally made a commitment to follow King Hertfa. This happened early in life before he was married, and he thought his life would change dramatically once this choice had been made. He did not realize or know that King Hertfa had a plan and a purpose for his life, and it was only going to be fulfilled when he made his own choice about staying loyal to the king or falling away to go after the dark lords.

King Hertfa was grieved when Herbance became disillusioned by the dark lords and took a stand against him. But King Hertfa knew this had to happen so that Herbance could become the willing instrument of the king. King Hertfa knew that it had to happen in this fashion. It did not make it any easier knowing that it had to be this way. The king mourned every time any of his subjects left his service to go over to the evil of the dark lords and serve them. This time of seeing his servants abandon him and go to the dark lords was a terrible time for King Hertfa. But he also knew that once they found out the truth and applied it to their lives, wonderful and marvelous things would come to pass in their lives and service to him again.

The king knew that Herbance was only reacting to the problems which he had experienced in his life. But this did not help King Hertfa with the feelings that betrayal had come to him through this man. Herbance created a position for service to King Hertfa believing that King Hertfa would come and help him with all of the problem areas in his life. What Herbance expected from King Hertfa was more than could be expected at such a time in his life but his youth caused him to think the king had abandoned him. It was easier to take the way out which was offered to him by Lustureus than to continue his service to the king. Service to King Hertfa involved more than Herbance was willing or ready to give. Herbance knew that he could not fulfill or complete this service to the king, so he stood by and waited for the dark lord Lustureus to help him with his decision about who he would serve. When Herbance realized that what he had envisioned for his life did not come and be fulfilled, he turned his back on the king. At this point Herbance stated to King Hertfa that he wanted nothing more to do with him in his life.

From this moment forward, King Hertfa was obligated to remove his presence and his authority and power from Herbance's life. The king did not do this willingly; he only did this when it was completely clear what the desire of his former servants were. But because of the circumstances and the way Herbance had made his desires clear to the king, his hands were effectively tied in the matter. The king had no choice but to allow Herbance to go over to the side of the dark lord Lustureus and serve him.

This broke the king's heart, as it always did when anyone decided to stop serving and fulfilling what they obligated themselves to the king, but this was the way the king approached this kind of issue. King Hertfa allowed the people to decide for themselves who they would serve, he let their free will become known to them and then to him in these matters. He did not retaliate against them or cause problems or ill will on his behalf. King Hertfa hated each time a dark lord was able to capitalize on some type of preconceived notion that the people had within themselves. He knew that once they had decided they would turn away from their commitment to the king, the dark lords gained another victory against him.

All King Hertfa could do after this kind of decision was to remove his protection from them and wait to see how long their service to the dark lords would last. The king knew that an alliance with the dark lords usually meant those who accepted this service within their ranks usually died while still serving them and being under their control. This grieved King Hertfa and he hated that this was the normal pattern for the people who turned against him and went into the darkness to live their lives. But he also knew that once they made their choice, it was up to them to change their decision and only then could he intervene.

Most of the people who willingly agreed to serve the dark lords never knew they had a choice in the matter. It is as if they make the choice to serve the dark lords and never understand the chance they have to change their mind again like they did when they left the king. They spend their days withering away until they passed from this life under the oppression and the authority of the dark lords. This saddened the king and made him feel like they needed someone to tell them that they could have a choice in their pathway in life. But alas, most never got the understanding that once they turned from the king and went to serve the dark lords, they could again change their minds and come back to service for the king.

King Hertfa often wondered why those who used to serve him, but now were serving the dark lords, never grasped that he would allow them to come back to his service. It was almost as if they thought that once they decided to turn away from serving him, their chance was over in life to ever reenter his service. King Hertfa could not understand why most of the people who fell from service to him felt this way. He only knew that very few ever got the courage and the desire to call on him for his help after they had gone over to the dark lords. Most people never realized that once they made a bad choice, they could make a good choice to follow it. This saddened King Hertfa and made him wonder what kind of monster most people thought he was.

King Hertfa knew that he was firmly in control of his empire and its people. Since he was unwilling to force his will on the people, he waited for the ones who had turned to the dark lords to come to their senses and see that they needed him. This process is what allowed the dark lords to maintain control and an unfair advantage in the lives of those who they were able to ensnare. King Hertfa was unwilling to advance on the people that the dark lords had established to follow them and most never knew they had the opportunity to return to him and serve him. This is why the king waited; it was not his will to force himself on any of his subjects. King Hertfa was willing to wait for them to see their need and then act upon it. This was the downfall of many of the people that the dark lords captured to follow them. They did not realize that King Hertfa was willing to take them back once they became disillusioned with their service to the dark lords.

THE BEGINNINGS OF NYKLONECI

It was a time of great upheaval in the land; many of these dark lords were out prowling around to find people that they could convince to follow them and help them take their stand against King Hertfa. Since the king was operating in his full capacity knowing that he was the ultimate authority, he would often ignore the dark lords. King Hertfa did this because he figured most people would eventually see the dark lords for what they were and return to serving him.

Herbance was the one who had chosen the dark lord Lustureus and began to serve him with all that he had. Herbance had become embittered because of his life and his belief that the king would intervene and change the circumstances in his life. Before he allowed King Hertfa time to react and respond to his request for help in his life, he made his choice. He became disheartened with his life and made the choice to turn away from the king.

Lustureus was the first one of the dark lords to come to him and offer him his services. Herbance had no idea what he was allowing into his life by accepting this proposal. But after he found what he thought he needed and wanted, he accepted and began to serve this dark lord with his life.

This is why Lustureus was so set on being able to control and influence the life of Nykloneci. He knew that once he had his father Herbance under his control it would only be a matter of time before he would control Nykloneci in the same way. The dark lords would often settle into a family and follow it along to see if they had a chance to embrace the next generation within their power and control. Many times it only took time and this seemed to be something that the dark lords had plenty of. They would wait and allow something to happen to the children and this would allow them to come to the rescue of someone in the family structure. Waiting for someone to find a new low place in life was their specialty. They were excellent at finding someone who was ripe for the picking.

Once this process started, it would give Lustureus the opportunity to continue to control and oppress the lives of others in the family line. It only took one who was willing to allow Lustureus to invade their life, and then it was only a matter of time until he was able to influence and control others in the family. Lustureus knew this was his chance to maintain some influence and keep his hand in the family line of Herbance. He would be able to cause any of his children to maintain in this alliance that would stand against King Hertfa if they were willing to allow him to do so. This pattern of behavior was able to be maintained for three or four generations at a time by whoever was in control of them. This was done by simply collecting the next generation and clouding their vision and maintaining the control which was needed to keep them faithful to what their forefathers had committed to. Lustureus was an expert at this type of behavior and he knew what he needed to do to maintain control over his servants. He was able to keep the people that he had convinced to follow him within the lines he had drawn for them in life. He was in firm control over Herbance and did all that was necessary to lay the groundwork to have a pathway to Nykloneci.

Lustureus gave his memories to Herbance and firmly implanted them within his mind. Herbance believed that he had committed atrocious things, even to the point of killing people with his own hands. Even though this was not true, Herbance believed what was imparted to him by the dark lord and these memories became his own. He saw himself traveling throughout the land of the king and doing these terrible things to the king's subjects. He even was able to transform himself into a monster that would feed on the flesh of his victims. These images were implanted within his mind by Lustureus, but they were as real to him as his own life. This is the power that the dark lords always implant within the mind of those who choose to follow them. They make their own memories real for their servants and use them against them to maintain control over them in this way.

Herbance had terrible nightmares about what he had committed against the servants of the king and these memories stayed in his mind after he awoke from these dreams. The memories of Lustureus were firmly implanted within his mind. Any time he would wander away from the path that Lustureus had in mind for him, these memories would immediately bring him back under his control. The anguish and torment would cause feelings of guilt and remorse that kept Herbance in line and under the firm control of Lustureus. It was almost as if Herbance no longer had memories of his own. It was as if everything in his mind was a direct reflection of what Lustureus had done in his life. This type of mind control and manipulation was what kept most people serving their dark lords. They became fearful of what they had become, even though they did nothing that they believed they had done.

This was the choice of Herbance, nothing was thrust upon him, and he made the decision to turn from serving King Hertfa on his own. This choice was given to all who served the king and he never intervened when this time of decision arose in the lives of his people. King Hertfa allowed the people to make their own choices as to who or what they would serve, and once they made their decision, he honored them. What most of the people who do this did not know or understand was that King Hertfa never shut the door on their ability to return to him. King Hertfa waited for all the people who made the wrong choice in life, with regard to who they would serve, to return to him. Most people never understood that the king was willing and ready to accept them back. It is amazing that once the servants of the king stopped serving him and followed the dark lords, their minds were never clear enough for them to understand this possibility. It was almost as if the door to their minds was shut and barred by the dark lords. These people never were able to grasp or comprehend that King Hertfa would once more allow them to come to him and seek his forgiveness.

This was the downfall of turning from the service of the king to go their own way. Most people found something else to serve. They never grasped that they had the chance to return to the king and his provisional help. All people choose their own pathway in life; this was their right and privilege. Herbance made a choice that lacked any wisdom for his life. But it was his choice and one which he had to acknowledge as his own. Herbance made his choice and he was determined to stay with his choice and live his life serving someone other than King Hertfa. This choice was a bad decision and the worst one that could be made. But Herbance did not realize how bad of a decision it was until he thought it was too late for him to change his mind. Herbance made the choice of his life and as a result, his life was changed beyond anything that he could ever imagine for himself. Herbance had effectively set the course of his life and he started on a journey that he

THE BEGINNINGS OF NYKLONECI

never understood or realized the possibilities. The choice was made and now the pathway was set for Herbance. He started his journey through life with Lustureus as his new friend and master.

Nykloneci's Early Years

With this diverse and novel set of parents, Nykloneci was born in a small quiet village and was raised for the most part by his mother. She attended to his needs and kept him safe in spite of his father. His mother took great pains to protect him and keep him safe because the dark lord of his father Herbance was a constant issue that had to be dealt with. Lucy knew it was her mission in life to watch over and protect Nykloneci from anything which might come into his life in a negative way.

The dark lord Lustureus would come and visit the household often. He would create problems for this family by invoking his will to be done in opposition to King Hertfa. Nykloneci's father had a regular job and was required to spend large amounts of time away from home daily to carry out the work to supply the needs of his family. The dark lord was in firm control of his life and this kept him occupied most of the time even when he was home with his family.

There was no way of knowing when the dark lord would appear in their home and demand attention from Herbance. Nykloneci took it all in a humble and ignorant posture. He truly did not realize or understand the hold the dark lord had over their household. Being a child, he did not worry himself

THE BEGINNINGS OF NYKLONECI

with those kinds of unpleasantries. His life was filled with playing and spending time alone or with his mother.

Nykloneci was a handsome boy and he had the cutest blond head of hair that was so common with the people of this village. Once they grew older, most of the children adopted the ways of their families and would gladly accept their place in life. Nykloneci was not subjected to his father and the service of the dark lord, because he was kept safe and apart from all of this by his mother; or so she thought.

The only issue which arose for Nykloneci was he began to understand what fear was and the hold that it had over his father's life. Nykloneci was about to witness some of what his father did in his service to Lustureus. This caused him to be very afraid of his father and to realize over time that his father was serving evil.

Nykloneci observed his father operating in the power of Lustureus when he would drink. When his father would drink, Nykloneci was subjected to verbal and emotional abuse which came from the effects of the dark lord. With his father being under this kind of control, the alcohol allowed Lustureus to manifest in his life in a way that caused Nykloneci to shudder in fear.

Nykloneci had observed his father manipulating fire and causing it to do things that were not common or ordinary. Many times Nykloneci would wake up from his sleep to hear his father chanting and lighting candles to practice his control of the flames. A few times he even got the nerve to leave his room and walk down the hallway to his father and watch him as he caused the flame to move up away from the candle and burn in mid air without any kind of support or supply. This caused him to shudder with fear and wonder what was happening to his father. When his father would do this it also caused Lustureus to come and attend these times of Herbance practicing with his power.

Nykloneci learned to stay away from his father when he was drinking. When he witnessed his father performing these rituals it brought a fear to him that he did not understand. He began to realize why he had this fear of his father and what he did during these times. He only knew that something was terribly wrong when this kind of thing happened to Herbance. These times gave him cold shivers that went completely into his bones. When he witnessed his father doing the chanting and moving the flames, he knew that his father was not in control—Lustureus was exerting his will on him.

Many times Nykloneci witnessed his father sitting in the living room drinking and relaxing late at night. He would see a vapor mist leave his father's body and travel out of the window. The first few times this happened, Nykloneci thought that he had imagined seeing this and wondered if his eyes were only playing tricks on him. But over time he realized that something was leaving his father to travel the world. When the vapor mist returned, his father would return to normal and sleep.

There were rare times when Herbance would talk about where he had traveled to and what he had done during this time of the vapor mist leaving his body. Nykloneci knew that something dreadful and dramatic was happening to his father, but he did not grasp what it entailed. He did know that when his father started talking about where he had gone, the chill of fear would run through him like it did when Lustureus showed up at their home. Nykloneci hated it when Herbance

THE BEGINNINGS OF NYKLONECI

started telling him about what he had experienced during these times of traveling during the night in the vapor mist.

Nykloneci had a normal childhood in spite of his father. There were only a few times when his father threatened him because of the desires of the dark lord Lustureus. There was one time that will be locked away forever in the mind of Nykloneci. Herbance had decided that it was time for Nykloneci to learn how to fish.

The day came and Herbance took Nykloneci to a small pond. They began to throw their lines into the water to see if they could have some luck fishing. The day went pretty well until suddenly Lustureus showed up and began to cause intense pain for Herbance. It was at this point Nykloneci became overcome by fear, not fear that most would ever realize in their lives. This was a deep fear, the kind which usually brings death with it. Nykloneci started trying to get Herbance to leave the pond and go back home. The fear which came over him was so overwhelming that he was shuddering and shaking because of this fear. Nykloneci knew when Lustureus came, he could feel his presence, and he could see the effects on Herbance.

This was one of those times when Lustureus came with a vengeance and Nykloneci begged Herbance to go home. Nykloneci knew that something terrible was going to happen if they stayed at the pond fishing. After the pain was inflicted upon Herbance, he turned to Nykloneci and told him that his life could be over in a very short time. All it took was for him to throw himself into the water and wait for the water to engulf him and take him to the bottom of the pond. Herbance also told him that if he was too afraid to do it himself, he would be able to throw him in and watch him sink into the depths.

Nykloneci knew this was the result of the control of Lustureus, but he was so afraid of his father at this point that all he could do was sob and fall on the ground holding on to a small tree. Nykloneci just knew that at any moment Herbance would grab him up and throw him into the water of the pond, and his life would end. Nykloneci knew that day, and he came to realize for some unknown reason his life was being held in the balance. He could not understand why, but he knew that if Lustureus had his way, his life would be over before it was allowed to go for long. Little did Nykloneci know or realize that the fear was the controlling factor which Lustureus was in need of to keep a close tab on his life to try to maintain some kind of control over him in the future. Fear overtook Nykloneci to the point that once they left the pond, he made a vow to himself that he would never go fishing again. There was nothing which could be done to get him in this situation again in his life.

This memory haunts Nykloneci even to this day. He will never be able to think about fishing without this fear becoming real in his life again. Nykloneci knew from this point forward his life was in extreme danger and he knew that he had to watch his step when Lustureus showed up from time to time. Even now whenever Nykloneci thinks about fishing, his heart begins to pound within his chest and his palms grow sweaty, and he begins to feel the fear growing inside of him. This memory has haunted his mind and dreams for years and will be with him throughout his life. Nykloneci has a terrible fear of drowning and when he has these dreams of dying in this fashion, he always wakes up in a pool of sweat and his heart pounding from the dreams. This is one area of his life where Lustureus was able to gain control and use this to bring the fear to Nykloneci when it was necessary for him to do so. This fear would always be a part of Nykloneci's life and it will haunt his dreams until his life is over. Nothing will ever be able to stop this fear from taking control of him when he remembers this one day and the ramifications of what happened during a time of fishing.

The fear which came into Nykloneci's life was a controlling fear that never seemed to leave him. He knew that his father was not the source of this fear, but he also knew that whenever his father Herbance was at home, the fear was present with him. This led Nykloneci to have an intense fear of the dark. When it became dark outside, Nykloneci would seek the shelter of their home and avoid the darkness. It seemed to him that when darkness fell, a cold eerie presence would come to him. This feeling grew as Nykloneci grew; it was almost as if the darkness held secrets that he knew would one day haunt him. Nykloneci still did not completely understand how the dark brought this fear to him. This fear was so intense in his life that when he went to bed at night, he would stay there until morning light. Nykloneci would often wake up during the night and need to go to the bathroom and pass the water that was growing in his bladder. But this fear would not allow him to get up out of bed and go down the hallway to the bathroom. Many times he would lie in his bed shivering from the vast amount of water that was contained within his bladder, but he did not dare to get up and travel the hallway.

Somehow Nykloneci knew that something was waiting for him in the darkness and because he felt this way he was always afraid of the dark. Many times he would go back into a troubled sleep only to awaken again with an extreme desire to go to the bathroom. If there was a hint of light he would timidly tiptoe down the hallway and relieve the pressure, but if darkness was still veiling his way, he would only try to go back to sleep. Once it became light he would run to the bathroom and he would spend a few minutes easing the pressure on his bladder.

Herbance would often tease him about this and ask him where he keeps all of the water for so long. This was another way Lustureus caused Nykloneci the pain and suffering from his father's words. There were even times when Herbance would time Nykloneci to see how long it would take him to empty his bladder and then comment on the fact to Lucy about how such a small boy could hold so much water within himself. This was embarrassing to Nykloneci; he hated it when Herbance would call attention to this. Nykloneci knew his fear of the dark was the reason he had to undergo this kind of treatment. Most children are a bit afraid of the dark, this is a normal part of the growth process, and over time they get past this fear. With Nykloneci, the fear of the dark grew right along with him; he was more and more afraid of the dark the older he got. Nykloneci knew the darkness was when the dark lords were active and this fueled his fear. Since he had witnessed his father displaying the power of the dark lords in the night, this instilled in him the fear that would never leave him. Fear of the dark was not only fear of the physical world around him. Fear of the dark also involved the evil power of the dark lords—this is what made Nykloneci shudder in the night.

Nykloneci grew up sheltered from most of the ranting of his father by Lucy and her constant watching out for him. Except for the times when his father would take him and spend time with him away from the village. Nykloneci had very few friends because there were no other children in the neighbor-

THE BEGINNINGS OF NYKLONECI

hood where he was raised. His father Herbance would only allow him to spend time with people that he thought would help to further the bad influences in his life. There was an older man who was considered by many to be the drunk of the area, and he would often stop by and gather Nykloneci up with his favorite toy and take him with him to the local liquor shop. This man would come by and see Nykloneci standing in the doorway of his house and stop and yell for him to come and go with him for some candy and treats.

The local liquor shop was only a stone's throw away from where Nykloneci lived, and with the thought of candy and treats, he was always ready to run out to him and go along. This man formed the habit of coming by to get Nykloneci a couple of times a week to take him along to the local liquor shop and he would bring Nykloneci back home with candy and a big smile. This man was the first friend Nykloneci was allowed to have, and Herbance and his mother Lucy saw no problems with him enjoying the company of this man.

There were directives that came, which were the direct result of the control of Lustureus in Herbance's life. Because of his mother's attention and protection, these times of spending time with his father were few and far between. The times spent with his father only served to instill the fear which was needed for Lustureus to gain access into his life.

Nykloneci was always a happy child when he was under the protection of his mother Lucy. He would laugh and play when she was around watching and interacting with him. He was always obedient to what she told him to do. This remained in place until the time for him to begin school. Lucy knew that changes would come, but she did not expect what happened once he found his new friends in school.

It came time for Nykloneci to attend the local school and learn all he needed to prepare him for life in the world. He did not really appreciate his education and would often make references to the fact that he did not need it for much. He grudgingly went to school and once he applied himself he came to understand the importance of his education. Like most children, he got bored easily and would daydream from time to time about what his future would hold. Many times he would envision himself as an adult with a wife and children. But something just never seemed to fit for him when he thought about his future. It was obvious that his life was marked, but he did not understand or grasp the implications of what lay in store for him. His imagination was one part of him that Nykloneci loved to play with, and once his imagination kicked in, he never seemed to know where his next adventure would come from. His imagination seemed to have a mind of its own and once it started, Nykloneci was along for the ride but not in much of any kind of control over it. This was the open doorway Lustureus needed and operated through to keep some control over Nykloneci. His imagination was a way for Lustureus to stay in contact with him without him realizing that this process was set in place and put in motion for him.

Nykloneci grew up normally and he developed some friendships that lasted for days, weeks, and years. He seemed to attract the children who were not in the main social circles. He seemed to grasp and understand that he would never be in those circles because of his standing and the work which his father Herbance did. Nykloneci realized that he would never have a high standing as long as he stayed in the small village. Nykloneci changed after he began to attend school and one

THE BEGINNINGS OF NYKLONECI

aspect of his nature became apparent. He did possess one dark point in his life; this was the time when he began to lie and to fabricate what he wanted to be true in his life. This lying began after he was out of the control and love of his mother, and when he started attending school away from home, the lying continued and grew.

It did not take long for his mother Lucy and father Herbance to realize that his lying was a direct result of his vivid imagination. His imagination was both his claim to fame and his downfall. Nykloneci was a brilliant child with regard to his imagination, but the lying which came out of his personality was a direct association with his father's dark lord Lustureus. He did not realize that this behavior allowed the dark lord access into his life. But over time the lying became an obsession that Nykloneci was not able to avoid or overcome. The lies that he told to cover his shortcomings would grow and develop in the same way as his body grew during those years. It seemed Nykloneci was subject to fabricate lies in order to maintain his life and this was the opening that Lustureus kept monitoring during his life.

The time came for Nykloneci to get his first pet. His friends from school all talked about their pets and how wonderful it was to have them. Nykloneci came to Lucy and asked if he could get some kind of animal to have for his own. Lucy tried to explain how difficult this was, and that if he truly wanted a pet, he would have to commit to taking care of it himself. Of course Nykloneci did not realize what this would mean to him, so he continued asking Lucy for a pet of his own.

Lucy talked to Herbance about Nykloneci's need for a pet and Herbance sat Nykloneci down to explain that it took lots of time and energy to care for another creature. Nykloneci had his mind made up—he wanted a pet and nothing else would do. Herbance asked him what kind of pet he had in mind, and he said a dog. Herbance told Nykloneci that once this decision was made and the pet was purchased and brought home, it would be his responsibility to take care of it—to feed and water it. Nykloneci agreed, much too eagerly and stated he would be more than willing to do this if he could only have a pet. Herbance took the time to put up a fence around the backyard of their home for the dog. He also sought out a craftsman to build a structure appropriate for housing a dog. Once this was accomplished, the time came for the search to begin for an animal that would be appropriate for Nykloneci.

Herbance and Lucy decided that a shepherd dog would be the best for Nykloneci, and this would hold his interest and give him an animal that would be smart and able to learn. The search began, and within a couple of weeks, a beautiful patchy dog was found with one dark eye and one light one. Nykloneci was very pleased with this dog, and he began to bond with her immediately. While the puppy was small and Nykloneci was able to control it and handle it well, things went smoothly.

Over the course of the summer, the dog grew, and it had a blue patchy coat that was dark, light, and had some white mixed in with it. Being a shepherding animal, the natural instincts took over after a few months, and whenever Nykloneci would enter the back gate, the dog would come to him and begin to move him along. This was great fun for Nykloneci at first, the dog would come up beside him and they would run and play together, and this brought great joy to Nykloneci. But after a couple of months, the dog began to take control of their time together. If Nykloneci would not go the way she wanted him to go, she would nip at him and show him that she was the one who was deciding what would happen next.

It did not take long before whenever Nykloneci would enter the fence, the dog would be there immediately moving him along the way she wanted him to go. She would bark and then nip at him to get him to move the way she desired. It was at this point when Nykloneci talked to Herbance about getting a chain to keep her by her doghouse. Nykloneci did not take the time to explain what was happening with the dog. He only wanted to be able to control her and keep her from taking control every time he entered the backyard. Herbance did not understand why Nykloneci felt this way, but he purchased a chain and proceeded to keep the dog tied to her house. It was at this time when Nykloneci grew tired of having a dog. He determined that if he stopped feeding and watering her, she would die, and then he would be free from the responsibility of caring for her.

Herbance would buy the food for the dog, and he began to notice that it was not going as fast as it used to go. He went out to see if the dog was being fed after a couple of days of noticing this and realized she was very thin and had a wild look in her eyes. He went and got her some food and took it out to her. He noticed she had no water in her bowl, so he refilled the water. When he placed the food on the ground, the dog ate as if she had not eaten in days. She also went after the water like she had not had any in a few days.

Herbance waited for Nykloneci to get home from school that day, and he asked him about what he had noticed and dealt with. Nykloneci told Herbance he had grown tired of the dog, and it was time to get rid of her. Herbance reminded him that he had made a commitment to take care of the dog and he had not done so properly.

It was at this point Nykloneci stated every time he let her loose, all she did was force him to move around the yard the way she wanted him to go. He was tired of this, and he did not want to turn her loose from the chain or play with her any longer. It was at this point Lucy saw this was turning out badly for everyone involved. She took over the feeding and watering duties for the dog until it could be taken to find a new home.

Lucy wondered why the care and feeding of the dog had gone the way it did. When she questioned Nykloneci about it while Herbance was at work, he told her about her nipping and herding him around the yard. He hated it when she did this and if he did not comply; she would force him to go the way she wanted him to go. Nykloneci even stated to Lucy at times she would stand in front of him and growl and then jump at him until he did what she wanted. This both scared and frustrated Nykloneci and he did not enjoy being treated this way by his own pet.

Nykloneci then said to Lucy he felt like his life was bad enough anyway with both of his parents telling him what to do. He did not need a dog to do this to him, and force her will on him too. Lucy listened to him, and then she made the decision that it was time for her to take care of the dog until it was time to find her a new home.

The day came when it was necessary to take the dog and remove her from her house. The dog had become angry with being chained up all of the time. She would not respond to Herbance or Nykloneci and would bark and snap at them when they got close to her. Since Lucy had been feeding her, she was the only one that the dog would allow to get close to her. It fell to Lucy to get the dog and put her in the carriage to take away. This broke Lucy's heart, and she cried and held the dog close to her as they drove along to take the dog to her new home. When they arrived and put the dog in the pen, it was a time of tears and heartbreak for Lucy. She had grown so attached to the dog after taking care of her for a couple of weeks that it was heart-wrenching for her to put the dog in the cage and then drive away. Lucy made the decision that day, no pet would ever be allowed for the family from that day forward. It was just too painful for her to have to do this again, so no pets would ever be allowed.

Lucy wondered how long Nykloneci would have gone without feeding or watering the dog. This made her wonder what had changed in his life to allow him to be so cruel. At this point she knew something was terribly wrong with Nykloneci. He had never behaved this way before, and she wondered how he could be acting like this now. Lucy spoke to Herbance about this and asked him why Nykloneci would do such an awful thing. It was decided that they should both keep their eyes on him for a while to see if this kind of behavior continued.

Lucy began to realize that a pattern was emerging with Nykloneci. It was one that she did not like or feel like it had any place in his life. If Nykloneci could be this cruel to his own pet, what else was he capable of that neither of his parents had seen yet?

The Growth of Imagination

The years passed, and Nykloneci developed much the same as any other child. He did have one aspect of his makeup that did not sit well with his parents. The lying was seen as only a phase that he would grow out of eventually. They had no idea that his lying was motivated and directed by the dark lord Lustureus to bring Nykloneci close to him and keep him under his control. Nykloneci was drawn to the dark lord through the lying, which he had developed and worked on to the point that it seemed he did not know how to tell the truth. Nobody knew or grasped that this aspect of his makeup was the one thread which kept the dark lord attached to his life. If it could have been recognized for what it was, things might have turned out differently for Nykloneci. This use of Nykloneci's imagination was paramount in his life and even though it was necessary for him to survive and carry out his destiny, this was also how he fabricated his lies. This truly was a double-edged sword that would carry him along in life and create problems for him which he would not be able to overcome.

Nykloneci learned that his imagination was a vital and important part of his life, and he would use it as much as possible. The imagination alone was not a problem, but with the way in which it was accessed by Lustureus, this became the problem. It helped him to pass the time because he was lonely.

THE BEGINNINGS OF NYKLONECI

As with most children, he needed some kind of companionship from someone his own age, but alas, there was nobody for him to bond with in the village.

The part of the village where his parents lived was populated by older people, and there were no children close by. This only resulted in allowing Nykloneci to use his imagination to create people for him to talk to and play with. He would spend many hours out in the yard playing alone and talking away as if several children were in the yard with him playing. It was out of this kind of activity that the dark lord had access to him and would come to visit him. He did not realize what the dark lord was or how he was able to invade his thinking and help him to form the imagination that he had. Over time, Nykloneci began to realize that his imagination was not normal or positive and that it was not truly his own.

Nykloneci knew that something was different about him once he began to let his imagination go and run wild within him. He realized quickly he was not thinking with his mind in the same way that other children thought. Nykloneci knew and understood his thinking was far advanced, but he did not fully grasp how this was happening at first. It took time for him to understand and come to realize that his thoughts were being controlled and steered in a way which was not bad, but somehow different than most people. When he was young, he did not think about his thought processes much. It just happened for him; and when it did, he would think and whirl about things that he came up with in his mind, but sometimes the things he thought of made him afraid. Nykloneci knew that his thoughts were more than just thoughts, but even with this understanding, he still did not grasp the full implications of the control and authority of the dark lord Lustureus in his life. When it came to imagination, Nykloneci knew that his was more active and better defined than most, but he still did not realize that he was not firmly in control of his imagination all of the time. This aspect of his makeup was the one place where Lustureus was able to interact with him and he did not fully grasp the consequences of how this was affecting him and bringing him closer to the dark lord. The power of his mind and imagination was the open door that Lustureus used to maintain his contact and control over Nykloneci.

Nykloneci continued to grow and develop, and his childhood was relatively normal except for the influence of the dark lord Lustureus in his life. The end result of this interaction was that nobody had the slightest inkling that this was happening. Even Nykloneci was not aware of the control and influence that the dark lord was taking in his life. He did know something was different about him, but the full evidence was hidden from him, too. The dark lord had the legal right and authority to come into his life because of the sworn service of his father. So the result of this involvement was not known for many years. This was the dark secret that was kept hidden from everyone who knew Nykloneci. But the result of this involvement was to be known later in his life.

Life continued, and Nykloneci was left alone with his thoughts and his imagination for many hours. This happened because his mother had decided that it was time for her to gain a vocation in the world. Since this was Lucy's desire, the decision was made for him to begin to be responsible for himself for about an hour each day. Lucy had to travel to a nearby city to get the training and education that she needed for her new vocation. She was only gone for about an hour of the time which Nykloneci was home from school, and she decided that this would be the only way for her to accomplish her goal in life of learning a trade. This allowed the dark lord Lustureus time to interact with Nykloneci without anyone around to suppress or observe this activity.

This bond grew tremendously during this time in Nykloneci's life, and the effect was not apparent to anyone because his great and imposing imagination was able to hide this involvement. Many times his parents thought that there might be some kind of problem with him and his thinking. But as he continued to learn how to lie and create the falsehoods that became an intricate part of his life, his tracks were being effectively covered by the dark lord, Lustureus. This intimate and problem-causing relationship was not realized until many years later when it affected the lives of many people who were serving the king. Nykloneci continued to grow and his imagination continued to be a source of frustration to him. He had ideas and thoughts that were not his own and this troubled him but he did not know what to do with them or how to avoid this kind of thinking. Over time he accepted that he was different, but he did not understand the significance of this issue in his life. But the fact remained that Nykloneci was destined for something great. He could not grasp or imagine the significance of this involvement with the king which would come later in his life. This tiny seed that had been planted within his mind was later to grow into an immense and terrible tragedy which would undermine his whole thinking and create a time of loneliness that would be unparalleled in his life.

The fear in Nykloneci's life grew as time passed. He could not understand why he was afraid or what he was afraid of. But one thing was certain; fear became an almost constant motivating factor in his life. He would often try to control his fear, but it was of no avail to any attempt that he made, it just seemed to be an intricate part of his existence. This fear was something that he tried desperately to manage and control, but it was not something that was natural or able to come under his control. Nykloneci decided that the fear would always be a part of his life. He accepted it as best he could and tried to continue with as normal a life as he could have, given the circumstances that he was brought up in. This fear was a motivating factor in his life, and the fear never seemed to leave him. Most times he could push it back in his mind and feel somewhat normal, other times it would spring forth and he did not seem to have any control over it at all.

The Course in Life Changes

It was when Nykloneci was eight years old that his father Herbance made a decision to break away from the control which the dark lord Lustureus had over his life. This was a tremendous and important undertaking because the dark lord had so much control over Nykloneci's father that he was not able to live his life without the influences which the dark lord would exercise over him. The time came for a decision that would transform his father's life, and when this happened it was a time of great and tumultuous problems for the family.

There was a holy man who came to the village where Herbance's family lived. This man had a unique and directional insight because he, too, had served the dark lord Lustureus. But this man had successfully broken the bond that Lustureus held over his life, and he knew that once he had broken free from this dark lord, he would be able to help others do the same thing. This man came to the village, and he set out to spread the word that he was a servant of King Hertfa now, but that he once served the dark lord Lustureus. With his incredible insight and former way of life, he was able to recognize and understand the problems which some people had by serving Lustureus.

Most of the people of the small village did not understand what this holy man was saying. Most had not given themselves over to Lustureus or served him like Herbance had done. But this man knew the torment and the torture that Herbance had endured because he had gone through it himself in life. This man actually understood all that had happened to Herbance and knew there was still hope for him if only he would denounce his service to Lustureus and begin to serve King Hertfa again. This man sought out Herbance and helped him to understand that he had options in life and the past bad choices could be reversed.

Herbance was filled with hope that just maybe he could actually break the power of Lustureus off of his life and remove himself from the bondage which he had willingly accepted. Herbance had reservations—it was unheard of for anyone to leave the service of a dark lord and survive. It seemed to be impossible to break free from the dark lords of the land and gain acceptance from King Hertfa again. But this thought came to Herbance, and he realized that if this man had done it, others could take the same pathway in life and be free again. This sparked an understanding that maybe it would be possible to break free from Lustureus and return to serving King Hertfa. Herbance had a hope that he had never had before, and it made him wonder what was possible for him to do.

Herbance made a bold step and asked the man to help him. Herbance explained that his choices had put him in this position in life, and now he knew that his choices were bad and wrong. The man said that it was possible to break free and again serve King Hertfa, but that it would be a process and not something that could be easily accomplished. Herbance gladly accepted this man's help and began to explain why he had made the choices that he had made in life. The man listened and admitted that he had done the same thing, and that

THE BEGINNINGS OF NYKLONECI

all it took was someone like him to help Herbance, and he would gain the freedom which he sought.

Herbance was overcome with emotions because of this wonderful information and being able to talk to someone who had gone the same way in life. The man agreed to help Herbance and he set about explaining what had to happen next. Herbance listened with intense desire and waited for Lustureus to appear and challenge this man. The man started telling Herbance about his own life and why he had made the same choice, and then he began to invoke Lustureus to come and be cast out of Herbance's life forever. This man was a holy man that came to the village where Herbance lived, and it was strange that nobody from this village knew who this man was. Another holy man who was just starting out in his vocation as a holy man with lots to learn had someone tell him that this man would come and hold meetings for him. This intrigued the young holy man, and he was happy to have someone who knew about the holy things to come and speak in his village. Nobody knew where this holy man came from, and once he left after a week of staying and speaking to the people of the village, it was as if he just disappeared. Nobody knew how to contact this holy man after he left, and many attempts were made to find him but all this effort was to no avail.

The time of waiting was short; Lustureus came quickly to this man's summons and proceeded to tell the holy man that he had no right to do this to him. The holy man immediately took authority over Lustureus in the name of King Hertfa and commanded him to listen and stop arguing his case. Surprisingly, Lustureus stopped short and listened to the holy man. Once the name of King Hertfa had been mentioned, Lustureus was not willing to do much arguing or stating his case any longer. Lustureus listened to the holy man, and once he realized that this was his old follower and he knew what he was saying and the authority which he possessed, Lustureus passively stood and listened for a few minutes.

The man explained that Lustureus had no control or power over the life of Herbance now and that King Hertfa had again claimed him as his loyal subject and follower.

With this, Lustureus shrieked and tore at his clothing and said that he would be back to make sure that Herbance was truly following King Hertfa. Lustureus stormed out of the room and made it plain that he would be coming back frequently to check on Herbance to see if his alliance with King Hertfa would stand and maintain.

Herbance gained a peace that he had not known before in his life. The assurance of this holy man that Herbance was now a servant of King Hertfa and not under the control or influence of Lustureus any longer began to soak into his mind slowly. The fear and intimidation were instantly gone and Herbance looked at this man with true humility and thanked him for his help and effort to set him free from the torture of Lustureus. This was a time of great celebration for Herbance; he was truly out from under the control of the dark lord, and his soul and spirit soared and swelled with love and happiness that he had never known before.

The fear of Lustureus was now abated and Herbance felt a new sense of self and was thankful for this holy man and for King Hertfa to accept him back as his humble and loyal follower. Tears of joy and gladness flowed from Herbance's eyes and coated his face as he was truly changed and would never be the same again.

The whole process was completed in one evening and Herbance wondered how his life would now change. He had so many questions and not many answers, but he knew that his life was now different and he would again be able to serve the king. Joy came to Herbance as he realized that his life was his own again, and if he remained faithful to his service to King Hertfa, it would remain this way from this day forward. Herbance was truly given a new chance at life and King Hertfa was willing to accept him back into his service.

This holy man who came to the village left that night after he performed what was needed for Herbance, and when he left many questions arose. It seemed that nobody knew who this man was, and when the people who had come to him and been helped by him wanted to know where he was from, nobody could answer their questions. Some people thought he was from an area many miles away, but others said he was not from that area because they knew many people in that area and he did not reside there. Even with all the questions, it became apparent that Herbance had gotten the help which he needed, and his life was changed. Herbance wondered who this holy man was and if he was truly a man or something else that only appeared to be a man. There was no way to contact anyone who knew this man or where he came from, so this part of what happened to Herbance still remained a mystery that was never solved. Herbance knew one thing, no matter who or what this holy man was, he was changed, and he was free from the control of Lustureus, and this was what mattered most to him.

The fear that was always a part of Nykloneci's life was intensified, and he did not know how to react to this fear. His father Herbance had always been under the control and influence of the dark lord until the time when all this changed. The change should have been a magnificent opportunity in life, but it did not work out that way. Over time, as the dark lord was no longer able to influence the life of his father Herbance, it seemed that he would come to Nykloneci and when this happened it would allow the fear to grow.

Nykloneci's father was subjected to many years of suffering and painful retaliation from Lustureus. At the time, nobody seemed to grasp or understand that the reason for this treatment was the attachment of the dark lord to Nykloneci. Everyone thought that the suffering was because Herbance had served Lustureus for so long that the tie which bound them together could never be broken. The people thought this tie between Herbance and Lustureus was strained, but not alleviated so they felt like this was a normal part of the process. But in actuality the reason for the visits from the dark lord was to check up on the growth and development of Nykloneci.

With his ties to Herbance, the dark lord knew that when the time was right he would be able to influence and control Nykloneci the same way in which he had controlled his father if he could remain in the background and bide his time. This tie was not realized by anyone in the family, and it was considered to be part of the growth process and what was necessary for Herbance to remain faithful to King Hertfa. Now that the dark lord was no longer in control of his father, the king realized that time would tell how Nykloneci would decide what to do with his life. Everyone felt like Nykloneci was able to go forward and do some wonderful things in life, but nobody grasped that the dark lord was still keeping a tight rein on his life.

Time passed and the visits from the dark lord would continue with devastating problems for Nykloneci's father Herbance. It was thought that something had gone wrong with his decision to stop serving the dark lord and begin to serve King Hertfa. The small village knew that something had changed with his father, but they all took the approach of waiting to see how long this change would last. Many times someone from this village had attempted to leave the service of the dark lords of the land only to fall back under their control. It was accepted that it would take time to see how things were really going and most would not commit as to what they thought about this matter.

Herbance knew in his heart that his time of serving the dark lord Lustureus was over. There was no way he would ever return to serving him once he had been given the chance to return to the service of the king. King Hertfa had accepted Herbance back into his service and began to allow him to carry out tasks for him. Herbance knew that once the king allowed someone back, it was not on a temporary basis. This was just another step in the journey of life and everyone waited to see what would come out of this latest attempt of someone to leave the service of a dark lord.

Many times Herbance would be home enjoying the peace that he had gotten from going back to the service of the king. He would be relaxed and in a state of wonderment about how wonderful the king was for allowing him to return only to feel that his old master was coming to see him. Lustureus would arrive at their home, and he would come in with force and bring fear and trembling to Herbance. There was no pattern to these visits, and when they happened it was something that could not be explained. One minute it was peaceful and quiet, and the next moment the air would become heavy, and then Lustureus would come and stand in the room barking orders at Herbance and telling him that he was back to stay again. Herbance would once again remind him that his hold had been destroyed by King Hertfa and that his allegiance was now to the king. Lustureus would glare at Herbance and listen to what he said only to add that when the time came for him to become an influence in his life again, he would know and grab the chance and things would change. Lustureus would always scream that he would always have access to Herbance and this would never change—it would only be a matter of time before things went back the way they used to be.

Lustureus would become angry and state once more that his hold would always be in place; there was no way in which Herbance could ever gain true freedom from him. Herbance would remind Lustureus that the bond was broken and that the holy man had set him free like he had been set free. Lustureus would go into a rage and start the attacks against Herbance and cause him to suffer physically with the blows that he inflicted on him. Herbance would often wonder how this was possible since the bond had been broken, but he did not realize that this treatment was only a side effect of the true visit. Lustureus was actually coming to see how Nykloneci was progressing in life. He would inflict pain and suffering on Herbance because without his knowledge, Herbance was allowing this to happen because he felt that he needed to pay some kind of penance to the king. Herbance did not realize or understand that these visits would only continue for as long as he allowed them. He truly did not realize or understand that once the bond was broken, it was broken for all time. Herbance knew that he deserved the treatment which he got

THE BEGINNINGS OF NYKLONECI

from Lustureus because he had left his service, but even he did not realize what the true agenda for these visits was until much later in life.

The true meaning of the visits was for Lustureus to remain attached to Nykloneci through his father. This was why Lustureus continued to come and inflict the pain and suffering which Herbance was allowing him to give. Herbance was free from the control of Lustureus, but in his warped thinking and his feelings of inferiority, he was allowing the dark lord to come and continue the punishment that he was subjected to. Herbance did not realize the bonding that had taken place between Lustureus and Nykloneci at this point, and he had no idea this was happening the way it was being carried out. Herbance only knew that Lustureus was not his lord and master any longer, so he considered what was happening to him as a normal part of the parting of the ways between them. Herbance knew that Lustureus would never again be his master, but for some reason he made no attempt to stop the visits that happened for many years. If Herbance would have gone to the king and explained the situation and asked for his help, the visits would have come to an abrupt end. But Herbance did not know that this was possible or a needed component at this time in his life.

King Hertfa set about giving Nykloneci's father Herbance standing within the community and he truly was a changed man. Nykloneci was not certain that his father had truly changed, but he wondered what the changes would mean to him and his life. It was almost as if he knew what to expect as long as his father was serving the dark lord, but with the new changes, he was uncertain about his future.

So Nykloneci took the same approach as most of the people in the village and waited to see if the changes would last or be a short-term situation for his father. Nykloneci knew that no matter what transpired, he would not change his life. In fact, he knew that his life would remain the same no matter what his father did. This was the element that kept the dark lord Lustureus coming to their home in the village.

Herbance thought that these times of testing and pain were only for his past service to him, but in fact these visits were also to check on the growth and development of Nykloneci. Lustureus was bound to keep track of the progress of Nykloneci and make sure that he had his tie to him left intact so when the time was right he would be able to control and influence him in his life. It was all a matter of timing and waiting for his time to be able to move into a position of control and bring Nykloneci to the point where he would make a decision to serve him. Nobody understood that this was what was happening in his life. With the passage of time, it became evident that Lustureus had a definite plan to use Nykloneci at a point later in life, but for the moment this plan was not revealed. Nykloneci changed from being the obedient and loving child who he had been to learning how to fabricate things and tell stories that were not true. Lustureus was an expert at waiting for the right time and the proper circumstance to bring his proposal to Nykloneci and see what he could get him to agree to and accept. This was the first step that Lustureus used in the life of Nykloneci. He helped him to learn how to fabricate things which were not true and stick to his story no matter how ludicrous it was. Nykloneci saw this as taking control of his world and setting things in place the way he wanted them to be. This ability was the starting point of the control that Lustureus was able to manifest in his life and the use of these made-up stories gave him a hold which he would build upon over time.

Nykloneci determined that no matter what happened he was going to set his course in life by his own standards. Little did he or anyone else know or realize that the dark lord, Lustureus, was already making his pathway in his life. It seemed that things settled down in his life, and his father changed in dramatic ways. The fear was still with Nykloneci, and he did not quite understand why but he felt like the fear was a part of him. So life took on a new meaning for Nykloneci, and he was trying to devote himself to the king and stay faithful to him, but the dark lord was exercising control over his life without his knowledge or understanding. Nykloneci made a conscious decision to serve the king and made this known to his father, Herbance. Herbance was happy that Nykloneci had finally decided that it was time to make a choice in his life.

Herbance instructed Nykloneci in the way that he needed to go so his service to the king would be noticed and acceptable. Nykloneci appeared to be listening and taking in what his father was teaching him, but something within him still wanted life to be his own way. This small spark that was standing in the way of his serving King Hertfa was not noticed or recognized for what it was at the time. Everyone was hopeful that Nykloneci was finally deciding to allow the king to come first in his life and begin to serve him faithfully.

Nykloneci realized that his life was going to change dramatically, and he wondered if this kind of change would be a good and useful thing for him or if it would take him away from his desires in life. Nykloneci knew that he needed to serve the king, but there was some small part of him that resisted this service fully. Nobody knew or understood that the control of Lustureus was alive and well in Nykloneci. It was the fear that he felt which was being used to hold him in check and keep him going the way that Lustureus had destined for him.

It was during this time of change that a dramatic incident happened to Lucy. She was on her way home from a neighboring city with supplies and food for the family. As she was coming home in her carriage, it suddenly went off of the road and ran into a tree. Lucy was badly bruised, and the supplies were thrown all over the carriage. Herbance was found and told about the accident, and he rushed over to the road to see what had happened. When he arrived, he saw the carriage off of the road and in the ditch up against the tree. He noticed that Lucy was limping badly and that she was in need of some help to get home. Herbance and the local constable asked Lucy if she needed medical care, and she refused.

Herbance helped Lucy to go home and got her to calm down and sit and unwind after her ordeal. Herbance asked what happened after Lucy had calmed down, and she stated that she did not know. One minute the carriage was on the road moving along smoothly and the next thing she knew the carriage was in the ditch up against the tree.

It was at this time that Nykloneci was having problems deciding how he wanted to live his life. He wanted to serve the king, but something inside of him wanted to go his own way. The time of decisions was still strongly on his mind and he was wondering if he made the right choice in serving King Hertfa. This internal conflict seemed to pull him one way at times and another way at other times. He was confused and did not understand why.

THE BEGINNINGS OF NYKLONECI

Two days after the terrible accident, while Lucy was asleep that night, a visitor came to talk to Herbance. This visitor came and announced that he was going to take Lucy away and that Herbance and Nykloneci would never see her again. When Herbance remembered how the holy man had called on the name of King Hertfa to stop Lustureus from arguing with him about Herbance, he decided to do the same thing in this situation. What Herbance did not know was that this was the chance for Lucy to pass from life into death without any lasting problems from the accident. Herbance was only thinking of himself and Nykloneci when he intervened in this process. His rash choice bound Lucy to him, and he would not allow this entity to take Lucy away. The visitor stated that Lucy was on his list, and he needed to take her away, but Herbance would not listen to him.

When Nykloneci woke up and heard his father arguing about his mother, the fear came to him in full force. He knew that something dramatic was taking place, but he was too afraid to get up and see what was happening. Herbance stood firm and would not allow the visitor to come close or touch Lucy, and she slept through the whole ordeal without waking up to hear what was happening.

The visitor was a small being with a dark cloak that covered his body. When he spoke, it sounded like a grating of items together that did not really sound like a voice at all. Herbance was sure that he would not allow this visitor to do what he was stating he needed to do.

After a lengthy discussion, the visitor finally stated that he would have to go talk to the king and let him decide what needed to be done next. When this happened, the visitor left and Herbance was left thinking that he may have made a grave mistake, at this point, but he was not going to let something like this thing take Lucy away. Herbance did not realize or understand this being was showing a kindness to Lucy. He only thought of life without Lucy and it was too much for him to bear after gaining his freedom from Lustureus.

The entity went to the king and explained what happened in full detail with Herbance's refusal to allow him to take Lucy. King Hertfa decided that Herbance could have his request in this situation, even though he knew it was not best, the king allowed this decision to stand. This entity was carrying out the orders of King Hertfa, but when the king heard the strong and forceful way in which Herbance had reacted, he allowed Herbance to gain what he wanted knowing that Lucy would suffer the rest of her life. King Hertfa was offering a chance for Lucy to pass from her life and gain what was waiting for her, but Herbance had effectively canceled the plans which the king had for her.

From the Village to the City

The time came for the family to move to a larger city and leave the small village behind. It was thought this move would be a definite improvement for all concerned, and it would bring about a fresh start in life. The move allowed Herbance to be closer to his work, and it would allow Nykloneci an opportunity to start over with new friends in a new place. There was even a thought that the visits from the dark lord Lustureus would stop once the move had been successfully completed.

The new house was filled with all the things that Herbance, Lucy, and Nykloneci had accumulated over the years. The move had gone smoothly and everything they had was placed in their new house. Things looked like they would finally settle into a normal pattern for them all. It did not take long for Nykloneci to rebel and state that he wanted to go back to the small village. He was not happy with life in the city, and he wanted to return to his old friends and his old school and what he was used to.

Herbance explained that it was not possible for them to do this, the old property was sold and their new life was here in the city, away from the small village.

Nykloneci flew into a rage and stated that he was not happy in the city and nothing would improve for him here, it was his choice to return to the small village. Herbance told

Nykloneci that this was not possible, and he was going to have to deal with it the best way he could and realize that changes come to all of us in life. It was only a matter of days before Lustureus showed up at the new house to show that he was still able to find the family no matter where they went. His tie to Nykloneci was so strong that he would be able to find him no matter where he went now.

Nykloneci now knew that these visits were going to continue, and he was happy that this aspect of life would not change for his father. It almost seemed to ease Nykloneci's fear when Lustureus showed up, and he was glad that his father would have to keep suffering from these visits.

Nykloneci secretly knew that with the continuance of the visits from Lustureus, he might be able to convince his father to return to the small village. Nykloneci did not realize at this time that the visits from Lustureus were directed more at him than his father. The pain and anguish continued for Herbance with each visit from Lustureus. Herbance did not realize that he could have put a stop to the visits any time he wished. All he needed to do was to implore King Hertfa to intervene and stop Lustureus from coming.

Herbance was a faithful servant of the king, but he also thought that he deserved to suffer at the hand of Lustureus because of all the time he had served him. In his mind, he thought that he could do penance for his sins by being subjected to the suffering which Lustureus brought to him. Even with a full pardon from King Hertfa, Herbance felt like he deserved what he was given by Lustureus. His mind was still clouded to the fact that this was not necessary for him to have to go through and endure. So the visits continued and the pain and suffering were allowed to continue. Nykloneci

THE BEGINNINGS OF NYKLONECI

secretly wanted the time of suffering to become so bad for Herbance that he would decide to move the family back to the small village. This was Nykloneci's hope, that if the visits from Lustureus continued, they would move back to the small village and his life could return to normal again.

Nykloneci felt like he had been uprooted and moved to this new city and all of his old friends were left behind. The truth was that Nykloneci had a comfort zone in the small village and, he only had a handful of friends so this part of his thinking was incorrect anyway. Nykloneci was more about being comfortable in the small village and the life that he was used to there. He did not realize the opportunities that would come with being in the larger city.

The first problem for Nykloneci was during the first week of school. The boys on the school carriage which he was riding on decided to find out how tough he was and confronted him and gave him his first fight. The carriage driver had to intervene and stop the boys from picking on Nykloneci and help him to understand that he needed to stand up to them but not engage in fighting with them. It was possible for Nykloneci to stand up to the problems in life without coming to blows, but this only drove Nykloneci to try harder to find ways to move the family back to the small village again.

Nykloneci began to look for ways to be able to force the family to move back. He did not realize that the property was already sold where they used to live, and there was no going back. This became an area where Nykloneci began to blame Herbance and Lucy for the changes in his life. He did not want things to change; he wanted to go back to the life he knew, and he was not going to stop until he got his way, or so he thought.

The real reason all this transpired was because Lustureus was not in sole control of the larger city like he was in the small village. Lustureus was the primary dark lord in the small village, and he was able to exercise his authority without anyone to stop him. The larger city had other dark lords who would confront him and try to stop him from operating within their territory. This was the primary motivating factor for Nykloneci; he was being used as a pawn to move the family back under the control of Lustureus. Even though it was more difficult for him, Lustureus made the journey to the larger city to intimidate and bring suffering to Herbance and check to see if he was being faithful to King Hertfa. With each visit from Lustureus, Nykloneci felt like his case for moving back to the small village was being reinforced.

The Next Problem Area of Life

Nykloneci went his way in life thinking that he was serving the king and going forward with his life. But the dark lord that his father used to serve had taken notice of him and set his sights on him in a powerful way.

This dark lord, Lustureus, was present in the life of Nykloneci without his knowledge or commitment but that did not hamper the dark lord from doing things in his life. The time came for Nykloneci to make some decisions. His mother Lucy decided that it was time for him to get some authoritative help in his life, so she impressed on him that he needed to enter the military service for the king.

Herbance had some ideas about this, too, but his ideas fell on deaf ears when he spoke to Nykloneci about what he needed to do. Nykloneci still blamed Herbance and Lucy for his problems in life. He just knew their decisions had made his life harder so whenever they mentioned something positive for him to do he would always ignore them.

Lucy began to suspect that something was not right with all the visits from Lustureus. Lucy knew that her husband had suffered a great deal over the years, but something was still amiss. Lucy decided that if Nykloneci was to be spared this same kind of influence and bondage, he needed some kind of discipline in his life. She knew that this had to come from someone who could enforce what they said to him. Lucy knew that Nykloneci would never listen to her or Herbance now, he was forming his own opinions of life, and he was starting to go his own way. She realized that her control over Nykloneci's life was coming to an abrupt and fast close. She wanted him to get the best possible help from someone who would be able to help him in ways she could not. Lucy knew that many times Nykloneci would wait until her eyes were off of him, and then he would do the things that most youngsters would do when they knew that nobody was watching them closely. He would do terrible things and cause problems for other people when he knew that his mother was not watching him.

Nykloneci was learning how to torture animals by moving close to them, and then when he got so close he would have a rock or two in his hand to throw at them and try to injure them. He would also go out in the backyard and scrape the soil off of the anthills and wait for them to swarm out to attack whatever was invading their homes, and he would stomp on them or pour water on them and watch them drown. One time, he saw a rabbit in the backyard, and he chased it until it became lodged in the fence; and once it did, he simply got a club and bludgeoned the rabbit to death. After he killed it, he left it hanging in the fence where it had gotten lodged.

He would often get caught by the neighbors because he was throwing rocks at their dogs and cats if they ventured too close to him. He even made a slingshot and began to shoot at the birds that were perched within range of him.

He began to destroy the furniture that Lucy had by cutting on the surfaces with his knife and cutting holes in the fabrics of the cushions. Herbance also noticed that there were times when he could smell alcohol on Nykloneci's breath. There were times when he would sleep for hours for no apparent reason, so he knew that his son was drinking with his friends.

He was caught by a local constable speeding along in his carriage in an area that had children, and you were required to move slowly through the area. He was charged a fee for operating his carriage without any kind of control and for driving it in a reckless manner. Even with these things happening in his life Nykloneci still had no regard for anyone or anything and when he was confronted with them he only shrugged them off. It was almost as if Nykloneci had no concern for himself or others now and this was taking him to a place where Lustureus could gain more control over him.

Lucy knew that this activity in his life had to come to an abrupt halt. The only way was for someone to be able to watch and monitor him around the clock and be able to enforce what they told him to do. Lucy hated that this drastic measure had to be implemented in his life, but Nykloneci needed some very strong and durable help, and he needed it quickly. Lucy knew that without some kind of help, Nykloneci would end up traveling the same pathway in life which Herbance had taken and this was not what she wanted for Nykloneci.

Lucy decided some military service would instill within Nykloneci what he needed to help him in life and give him the guidance and direction that he needed. She talked with Herbance about this, and it was determined that Nykloneci would benefit greatly from some kind of service to the king. Lucy set about helping Nykloneci decide what area of service he would be best suited for, and she decided that he would be best helped in the army of the king. Lucy settled this in her mind, and once she talked to Nykloneci and explained how this would help him, it was decided that he would sign up and join the military service.

Lucy made all the arrangements and got Nykloneci signed up and even took him to the station so he could travel to the location which was decided on for him to enter the military service. Lucy made certain that there would be opportunity for Nykloneci to gain some positive steps toward his education. The military personnel explained to her that they would allow Nykloneci to take some classes toward a trade if he was willing to sign up for them and do what was necessary with the classroom assignments.

Nykloneci had no desire to further his education, he only wanted to be his own person, and he saw this as a chance to get out from under Lucy's thumb. This decision for Nykloneci to enter the military service seemed to be the answer to his problems in life from every aspect. Nykloneci went off to begin his training for the military and everything seemed to fall in place for him. Lucy would write Nykloneci and inquire about how things were going, and ask if he was signed up for any of the classes that the military offered.

Nykloneci would write her back and tell her that they did not offer him classes. Nykloneci would explain that with his schedule of working times, it would be impossible for him to take the classes they had mentioned to her.

Lucy felt like he was telling her the truth about this situation, and she began to become embittered toward the military. They were making commitments that they did not keep to her and Nykloneci. She felt like the military had misled her in the opportunities they might offer to Nykloneci. This led Lucy to think she had made a terrible mistake by sending Nykloneci off to the military because it seemed like they were not able to help him in the way she expected them to be able to do.

The truth was that Nykloneci did not attempt to sign up for any classes, and he wanted nothing to do with furthering his education. Being away from home, he did not have to listen to Lucy and submit to her desires for him. He felt a freedom which he had never had before, and he wanted this to continue in his life. It became easier and easier for Nykloneci to submit falsehood after falsehood to his mother and father. With him being so far away, they had no way to check and see what was happening with him. This idea intrigued Nykloneci and helped him to begin to see how he was able to get what he wanted from his parents without being under their control. This new thought for him was extremely exciting and fulfilling because he knew that he would finally get to be his own person, since he was away from home.

Once Nykloneci was taken to the place for his service to the military to begin, he came to realize that he would be away from the control of Lucy totally. This inspired Nykloneci to take this newfound freedom and live his life his own way. He knew that his mother would not know about his day-to-day life. She would know about the things that he told her about, but not that he had decided he would do what he wanted as he wanted. The rebellion against his mother's desires for him had begun. She would never know what he was doing or what he wanted in life from now on. He was his own person, and for the first time in his life, he was not under her control or watchful eye. Nykloneci went through some regimented military service to his country and thought he was on the road to serving the king. But the dark lord Lustureus was still influencing his life in a very dramatic way. Nykloneci did not grasp what was happening to him, and he felt like his life was moving forward. As with most people, he was content to go along the river of life and float along without much direction or decision about his life. He found a girl during some maneuvers which were mandated by his military service, and he made every attempt to find out all he could about her. Nykloneci had his own carriage while serving in the military, and he formed a plan to be able to afford to go and meet with this girl in her city. The problem was that he had no money to be able to afford the trip. It would take several days for him to go there and meet with her and then to return to his military post. He needed money because he spent all of his on frivolous things that he felt like he needed to entertain himself during the off hours at his position in the military.

Nykloneci was forced by Lucy to keep a tight control of his money while he was at home. Now he could do whatever he wanted to do with the money that he earned. Nykloneci decided he would get the latest gadgets and items for his enjoyment and not worry about saving his money. The military supplies most of his needs, and they did not pay him much anyway, so why should he save money when there were so many things he wanted? Nykloneci spent what he was paid as fast as he got it, and he would entertain some of the other military people by sharing his treasure of gadgets and trinkets with them for amusement. He loved that Lucy was not looking over his shoulder now, and he was free to decide for himself what he wanted and needed to do.

It was during this time of serving in the military that Nykloneci met Darius, and they were the worst enemies when they first met. Darius was loud and boisterous and this did not sit well with Nykloneci—he could not understand why this guy had to be the life of the party and get noticed everywhere he went. They were assigned to do the same job, and over time their confrontation became something that was unsettling to Nykloneci. He finally decided that it was time to have it out with Darius and see what it took to bring him under control. They both hated each other but as time passed they both realized that they could not get away from each other and they fell into somewhat of a truce.

Over a short period of time they started talking civilly with each other and realized that they were both loners and they did not have many friends. One thing led to another, and before long they started looking forward to their time of working together and they became close friends. Nykloneci did not understand it at the time but Lustureus was bringing them together so that Darius could be a part of what needed to happen later in life. Darius was a hard-headed individual who had to have things his way or else he wanted nothing to do with you. Nykloneci was looking for someone to spend time with who would be willing to allow him to invest some time together. So this unlikely pair became friends and settled their differences and spent time together while they were serving in their military duties.

Nykloneci determined his plan to get what he needed to make the trip to see the girl he had met while on maneuvers for the military. Nykloneci called his mother Lucy and explained that he needed some work done on his carriage, and he needed money to get the work done. Lucy asked him how much he needed to fix his carriage, and when he told her she sent the money to him right away. She saw no need for Herbance to be involved with her decision, and it was her choice to decide if she would help Nykloneci. Nykloneci deceived his mother into giving him the money needed to make the trip to see the girl he had met. Nykloneci thought how easy it was to deceive his mother without her being there to look at him and see if he was lying or telling the truth.

Nykloneci placed this thought in his mind that whatever he wanted to do, he could ask his mother Lucy for what he needed. For the most part, he was sure he could convince her to help him. This decision set him up for a life of agony and frustration which he could never imagine. The dark lord Lustureus was clouding his vision and keeping him from seeing what his true purpose was in life. The lying was the tie that bound him to Lustureus and one which would not easily be broken. The longer Nykloneci went with the lying, the harder it was for him to tell the truth and this was all part of the plan for him. Lustureus was intent on keeping him going down this pathway in life.

Nykloneci made the trip and visited the girl, spent time with her, and he decided that when his military service was over, which would only be for a few more months, he would move to her city and plan from there. When his military service was over, Lucy wondered what Nykloneci would plan to do and if he would come back home to live and find a job. She had no idea what Nykloneci had done with regard to the girl, and she did not know about his plans to move to her city. The time for Nykloneci's military service came to a close and he had spent three years doing what he was told to do and living his own life.

Nykloneci knew that he had been successful in keeping Lucy in the dark about his opportunities in the military. He felt exhilarated with knowing that he had not done anything that she wanted him to do. With his time of military service over, Nykloneci moved back home with Lucy and Herbance. He realized that he could not stay long with them because they kept asking him about staying and finding a job to be able to support himself in life.

When Lucy asked Nykloneci how much money he had saved over the three years he was in the military service, he knew that she would not give up until he told her. This was an embarrassment to him because he had to admit that he only had a few hundred dollars saved after the three years. Lucy could not believe he had wasted so much of his money, and she sat him down to explain that he should have saved what he got from his service instead of wasting it on the junk he bought. Nykloneci knew that he had to leave soon and get away from Lucy; she just did not understand him. The time came for him to pack up his meager belongings and move to the city where the girl he had met and spent time with while he was still in the army was living. He started looking for a way to move his things, and when he calculated the cost of what it would take to move, he was horrified. Things cost so much, and once he acquired the means to move, he would almost be out of money once he got to the city where he was going to live. He contacted the girl, and she stated that she would speak to her father to help him once he got to the city. She would lend him some money and help him acquire a place to live.

Nykloneci proceeded with his life and moved to the large city where this girl was from. He was successful in finding a job of guarding a property for a lord of the king. The time he had spent in the military service was the perfect answer to the questions surrounding this position of employment. This allowed him to be close to his new love, and eventually they fell deeply in love and moved in together. They determined that they would try to see how life would be when they moved in and began to act like they were married. This proved to be a time of intense and wonderful intimacy for them both, and they engaged in every activity which they could come up with in the hopes that it would strengthen their relationship. Little did they know or understand that this was another ploy by Lustureus to show both of them the good side of life without the responsibilities of what was needed by them both. They both enjoyed the bliss of being together and experimenting in all the ways that a newly-formed couple would, but hidden in the background was the fact that neither of them knew what lay ahead for them both. This time of no responsibilities but all the pleasures of life did nothing to prepare them for wedded bliss. In fact it drove a wedge between them because they both knew the pleasures of life without the commitment that was needed for them to survive in the world together.

Nykloneci was without the means of providing for his new love, and he knew that she would need the necessities of life. He was also told by her father and mother that she was spoiled with regard to worldly things, and it would take a lot more than he could provide to keep her happy. Once he had this information, he knew that he needed a way to begin their new life together with the best possible start they could have.

Nykloneci knew that his new love would never be satisfied living in the place where he was staying, so he had to figure out a way to provide for her as quickly as possible. He followed the guidance of the dark lord, Lustureus, and used deception to get the means for their house in this large city. It was a cleverly concocted lie which he would use to gain the house in the large city, and he would use deception to

THE BEGINNINGS OF NYKLONECI

get his father Herbance involved with its purchase. Nykloneci told his father that his carriage was his only debt and that if he would be willing to help him by paying for it, then he would be able to get a home in the large city without a large upfront payment as there were many homes that were unoccupied there. Nykloneci even carried this ruse so far as to say that many people in this large city were now buying houses without any kind of upfront payment and that it was possible to do this. He even expanded on this line of reasoning to say that with so many properties being available, it was possible for the buyer to state the terms of the purchase with the seller and gain some wonderful concessions. Since Herbance had no idea that this was not possible, he believed Nykloneci and started telling Lucy that they should do what they could to help their son and his new wife to start their new life together.

Herbance was trusting and believed him because he was hoping that Nykloneci was a changed man and he could trust his request and proceeded to give him the money so that his carriage would be paid off. Nykloneci used this deceptive course to gain the funding needed to get a house in the large city. Since it was so far away, his father did not travel to this place to see what was coming to pass. Nykloneci used the leading of the dark lord, Lustureus, to gain his father's trust and get him to believe a lie to get what he wanted and needed in life. But as with most things that happen with the help of the dark lord, it was only a matter of time before the marriage fell apart, and Nykloneci was left alone in the world again. Nykloneci did not grasp that all of the things that had happened to him so far were a direct result of the influence of Lustureus. This influence was to be a determining factor in his life without him realizing the full extent of this control which the dark lord was exerting in his life. Each new turn in his life became another chance for the dark lord to exercise his authority in Nykloneci's life.

The truth of this whole experience was that his new wife's father had taken the time to explain and express to Nykloneci that his daughter would never be happy with him. He further explained that marriage would be the worst possible thing that could happen because his daughter was spoiled by him and his wife. They knew that she would never be happy with a common life again. The girl's father and mother were highly respected and acclaimed people in this large city. They worked in the upper echelon of the established hierarchy of this city. The fact that her father took the time to warn Nykloneci what would lay ahead for him did not change his decision. Love can make people blind, deaf, and dumb with regard to the aspects of life, and in this case, all the factors were in place to set Nykloneci up for what the dark lord had in store for him.

This failure of the marriage was a product of what kind of control and guidance the dark lord was using over Nykloneci's life. This was the turning point in how he would be able to gain control over him in time. The marriage was just another failure that would impact Nykloneci and make him weak so that when the proper time came, Lustureus would triumph and take control of him. The plan that Lustureus had formed was coming to pass exactly the way he wanted it to go. All he needed to do was wait for a low point in Nykloneci's life to spring into action and offer his advice and help.

Service to the King

Life seems to take many directions at the same time, and it is up to us to decide which pathway we will follow. Nykloneci followed the pathway which was set by the dark lord even though he had no inclination that the dark lord was exerting this kind of control over him. It was during this time that he got back in contact with his father Herbance and began to try to serve the king. Herbance went to the king to ask that he provide and bless the life of his son, Nykloneci. The king was doubtful that Nykloneci was ready for this undertaking and he expressed his concern to his father in no uncertain terms.

So it came time for Herbance to give his pledge that he would instruct and guide Nykloneci so that the king would see the desire of his son to faithful service. Nykloneci's father gave his pledge to the king that whatever happened with Nykloneci, he would be responsible and take the blame or the blessing as time would show with his service to the king. King Hertfa reluctantly agreed that once Herbance gave his pledge, he would allow Nykloneci to learn the ways of the servants of the king. This started the long road which Nykloneci would have to travel to grasp and understand what the king wanted and needed for him to be in his service. Herbance knew that whatever the outcome of Nykloneci's life, he would be held accountable for any actions or misgivings that came to pass.

Herbance also knew that King Hertfa had only allowed this great undertaking to come to pass because of his current standing with the king.

The training started with Nykloneci being instructed by his father Herbance in the service to the king. This was an intricate and wonderful time for Nykloneci and he began to understand what service truly meant. His desire to serve was potent and ready to be shown to King Hertfa. The king was still apprehensive with this approach and made it known to Nykloneci's father that he was still too young to be trusted with the secret things and the knowledge that he would need to serve effectively. Herbance continued to speak to King Hertfa about Nykloneci and assured him that he would become a willing servant. The king knew that Nykloneci was capable of many things, but he kept bringing up the issue of his youth. Herbance assured the king that he would instruct him carefully and fully so that he would grow in his understanding. King Hertfa finally agreed to allow Herbance the chance to teach Nykloneci in the ways of service.

King Hertfa was reluctant, but he knew that Herbance was now in a position to ask him for some special things and they would be granted. This was a wonderful time for Herbance and Nykloneci. They began to pick up their lives again and enjoyed sharing time together and learning from each other. Life had given them another chance to become close and to share their lives again. This was something that Herbance never expected to happen, and he was truly grateful for it. Herbance was happy to have his son back in his life in a wonderful and loving way, and he was determined to help him to learn and understand the ways of King Hertfa. What neither one knew was that Lustureus was still in the background waiting and biding his time for the chance to get involved with Nykloneci in a very real way. But for the moment, Herbance and Nykloneci were happy to be speaking and spending time together like they had not done in many years.

Learning from the Elder

It was at this time that Nykloneci's father had attained the level of elder to the king. Herbance had been in service to King Hertfa for twenty years and he had proven faithful in every way to the king. Since his turning from serving the dark lord Lustureus, the king had been diligent to keep Herbance busy in his service. Herbance had proven himself to the king by accepting each new task without reservation. King Hertfa knew Herbance would always follow him now with the freedom that he was granted from Lustureus being fulfilled.

Through the last twenty years of dedicated service, the king determined that Herbance should be made elder in his service. This is an honor which is bestowed on someone who proves their service and following to King Hertfa. It is gained through many assignments and much time of being directed to perform all the things the king needs to have done. This honor does not come by any other means. It must be earned through dedicated service and a willingness to follow all of the king's instructions to the letter. It takes years of complete service and the willingness to carry out your assigned tasks for this option to become available to anyone in the king's service.

Herbance never refused anything that the king asked and this allowed him to advance and achieve much more than most did in their service. Herbance was one of the few servants of King Hertfa who would take on any task for the king without even knowing what the task involved. This kind of service was rare and hard to find with many of the servants of King Hertfa. Most of the king's servants only performed what they chose to do and never without a full accounting of what each new task involved and required of them. Herbance was the exception to the rule of most of the king's servants. He would willingly accept any assignment which King Hertfa gave him without question.

You have to understand that many people serve the king, but their service is only a partial commitment to the king. Most people who serve King Hertfa are only willing to do so much in their service to him. They effectively draw the line in the sand and commit to a certain level and no more will ever be offered by them to the king.

Herbance had never refused the king in any matter that arose. He was totally committed to serving the king—no matter what the circumstances dictated. King Hertfa knew that this level of commitment was rare and did not come easily for most of his followers. There are many who serve the king faithfully and do all that they commit to perform for the king. This kind of service is necessary to show your willingness to serve the king, but there are those who are willing to do all that the king asks. These are the ones who achieve the positions that only the king can grant. Their service has been judged, and they have been found faithful to do all of the tasks which the king asks them to do. Only those who prove themselves to be exceptional and willing to perform any task which the king requires are given the position of elder in service to the king. These positions are the symbol of their service to King

Hertfa, and once they have been given this standing with the king, they have achieved a position of advisement to the king.

Herbance was one who had proven himself through the twenty years of serving King Hertfa. He never refused to do what the king asked him to do, and this was his greatest accomplishment in life. Lucy knew that Herbance put his service to King Hertfa first in his life. She understood that this was his course in life, and she accepted that he would always serve the king first—no matter what happened.

There were times when this was unsettling to her that Herbance would place whatever the king asked in first priority in his life. Many times she wondered if she would ever be given the chance to be first with Herbance, but she realized that this would never be the case. The feelings of bitterness were instilled in Lucy once she realized that her hopes and dreams of being the first priority in Herbance's life would never be fulfilled. She began to understand that her life would never have the meaning that she desired, and this made her begin to feel like her service to King Hertfa had all been in vain. Lucy started to blame the king for the issues in her life, and she slowly and steadily started to withdraw from the king in a very subtle manner.

Herbance was committed to the king first and foremost in his life, and Lucy resigned herself to this over the past twenty years and understood that this would never change. There were times when it caused her painful suffering to accept that she would never hold first place in Herbance's life. At times she was sorry that her place would always be second at best. This made Lucy feel like she was unfulfilled in her life, and she became a person who needed to be noticed. This brought Lucy to the place of doing all she could to attract attention to herself as often as she could. She would be loud and boisterous at times, and she would draw attention to herself by her laughter.

This also caused her to socialize with as many people as she could and because of this she was always looking for someone to be her friend. When she approached someone to be her friend, it was always a one-sided concern, and the person who tried to befriend her was always left hanging in the balance. Lucy was not able to keep friends because she would place too many demands on the friendship and this would drive people away from her. Lucy was one who was difficult to deal with—she was so demanding of people that this often drove them away from her. She tried desperately to make friends only to drive them away with her incessant needs.

Lucy was never able to keep anyone as a close friend for long, and this caused her to begin to desire her way in many areas of life. The seeds of bitterness were starting to be sown into the life of Lucy, and she did not realize or understand why this was happening to her. This marked the place in her life where Lucy needed things. She began to desire to get what she wanted and nothing else mattered to her now. Lucy realized that her life was not going the way she had planned so it was up to her to begin to bring her life into the focus and attention that she needed. Lucy began to realize that her life would be a lonely pathway that would bring her no help and no acceptance in the world. This is where she began to realize that if she wanted things, it was up to her to get what she wanted and for this, she needed money. Lucy began to see money as the answer to all of her problems in life, and this drove her to get all that she could. Her focus began to be on the money that she needed to get what she wanted in life. It seemed that nothing else really mattered to her anymore—only that she got more money.

King Hertfa knew the heart of Herbance intimately and would accept his word when he gave it concerning anything that he wanted to do for the king. So Herbance asked the king to allow him to acquire the knowledge that he would need to grow and serve the king. It was during this time that the king allowed the elder to give a gift to his son that would greatly help and influence his life. There were choices that had to be made and the choice would fall to the elder for his son and there were three gifting options to choose from. The first was sight, the second was feeling, the third was sensing.

The elder already had the gift of sight and knew that this would not be a tremendous help to Nykloneci, so he chose to give him the gift of sensing. This gift from the king would allow Nykloneci to be able to sense what was happening around him without seeing or feeling it. The gift of sensing would help to guide him along his pathway of serving the king. Nykloneci and his father, the elder, did not realize that this was all a grand scheme that was created and administered by the dark lord, Lustureus, to try to get back at the elder because of his turning away from serving him many years ago.

So Nykloneci and his father began to interact, and this gave the king some satisfaction in knowing that the elder had given his word to watch and guide Nykloneci in his growth and service to the king. It was a wonderful time for the elder because he had lost touch with Nykloneci and wondered if their relationship would ever be restored, as the elder started his son's training. This went well for a few months, and Nykloneci began to feel like he truly had found his place in life with his service to the king.

THE BEGINNINGS OF NYKLONECI

But there was a cloud on the horizon that was slated to grow and develop, along with the training which was being given to Nykloneci. How this went unnoticed by both Herbance and Nykloneci is still a mystery that may never be answered. Lustureus was still waiting for his chance to get control over Nykloneci, and he was biding his time. Things were being put in place and set in motion in such a way that only the king knew all that was happening. It is almost as if the eyes of Herbance were closed to this vast undertaking because if he had known, the training would have stopped immediately. Nykloneci continued his education with his father, and he began to understand what needed to be done for the king in his life of service.

The king has set one stipulation that had to be observed with regard to this teaching and training time. Nykloneci was only allowed to go where his father had been. There was no place where he could travel or experience that would fall outside of the realm which the elder had already been to and experienced for himself. This safeguard was put in place by the king so the elder would be able to follow Nykloneci to any area that he traveled to and be sure to investigate anything that happened while he was in the training stage of his development.

The elder agreed to these conditions with a promise and a gift from the king. The promise was that he would train Nykloneci in all of the ways of the king but only what the king would authorize for him to learn. The gift was the presentation of a cloak which would shroud the elder and keep him from being noticed by anyone that he would encounter during the time of training for Nykloneci. In this way, the elder could keep close track of all that Nykloneci would do and he was able to follow him without his knowledge as per the agreement which he had made with the king.

So it was set that the elder would wear the cloak and follow the exploits of Nykloneci during his training without his knowledge. The king had insisted on this arrangement so nothing would go on that was contrary to his plan and purpose. Herbance agreed and followed his promise to the letter and did all he could to guide Nykloneci in his growth and service to the king. Herbance knew his son would be extremely upset if he knew that his father was able to follow his every move. He did not mention this was possible or that it would be done during his training. Nykloneci was filled with an excitement and exuberance because he now felt like he was going to be able to serve King Hertfa in a new and wonderful way. He was beginning to think that his life would now have purpose and a direction that would be a wonderful and fulfilling experience as he learned what he needed to know to serve the king.

But as is the case with most people who rise to greatness, it was not Nykloneci's hopes that were fulfilled but the hopes of his father, Herbance. Every authority figure always has some aspirations and ideas they want to have accomplished by their subjects, and the king was seeking someone who would be able to carry out the missions that he had for them.

Herbance decided that his son Nykloneci was the one who would serve King Hertfa as a leader among men. This was truly a great aspiration for Herbance because of his past service to the dark lord Lustureus. But all of this changed one day when Herbance realized that he had the chance to return to service to King Hertfa and leave his old ways behind. Herbance

THE BEGINNINGS OF NYKLONECI

accepted this chance to become a servant of the king and he applied himself faithfully to King Hertfa. Herbance wanted great and wonderful things for his son, Nykloneci and it was up to him to help his son in his rise to greatness.

Learning to Control the Storms

The first step in the process was for Nykloneci to begin to understand how to control aspects of natural things and learn how to control them in their natural elements. This process started with an interest in learning how to control the weather and the lines of storms. There are pathways that storms follow because of the magnetic and geographic locations that mark the places where the storm tracks move. Once this information was given to Nykloneci and he could understand how they worked, he was given the task of trying to control weather patterns and storm tracks.

This part is very easy once you understand how these things work and what laws apply to them. Since the elder had learned how to use this kind of energy to manipulate the storm tracks and cause changes to the weather patterns, it was plausible that Nykloneci would learn them, too, and apply them as needed. There are times when it is very important that things be allowed to progress as needed, but at other times these things can be changed or modified to fit what needs to be done.

It is possible to stop a storm from going the way it normally would if there is a good reason to divert it to another location. This is not done at the whim of the person who modifies these processes. There has to be a specific goal and reason for changes to be made, and once these are identified, they are allowed to come to pass. Many times the storms acted as cover for the dark lords and their servants to accomplish what they wanted to get done. This was the primary reason that it was imperative because controlling the weather could change what these servants could do.

After understanding the whole process and how it all worked, it is possible for someone to control the weather and cause changes that would not occur naturally. The process is a simple one where the person involved only has to focus their energy on the event that needs to be changed. Once the focus is organized and implemented, it only takes a gentle movement to bring the storm to a different track than it normally would take. This is accomplished by speaking the change in the storm track into being and allowing the words that are spoken to change the track of the storm and bring it under the control of the person who needs to make changes to the storm track.

The main ingredient in this kind of control is the ability to clear your mind of any outside distractions. It was imperative that you focus all of your thoughts and energy on the storm and bring it to where you need it to go. Even though this sounds like a relatively simple process to bring to pass, it takes enormous energy and tremendous concentration.

The ability to clear one's mind and not allow anything to distract them from what they are doing is the key ingredient, but this ability does not come quickly or easily. It takes months of retraining your mind to focus and not allowing any distractions to come in the way of what you are trying to accomplish. Most people will not be able to focus this strongly; it takes your entire mind working in the formulation of what has to happen to begin the process. Any interruption will cause your focus to be interrupted, and the storm will return to its normal route.

Once this happens, the dark lords are again able to bring about what they set out to do in the wake of the storm and nothing would be changed. It is imperative that once you begin to control a storm track and hold it in a position that does not allow it to follow the normal course; you have to complete the process to bring about any change. Total concentration is needed to perform this endeavor, and only those with trained minds can accomplish this feat. It normally takes years of practice to be able to affect any kind of change to the storm pathways, but with intense effort it can be accomplished in a much shorter time frame. King Hertfa allowed Nykloneci to gain the understanding of how this all worked and to focus his mind because of the work of the elder. This was not the normal pattern of learning, but as Herbance kept insisting to the king, it was needed and necessary if Nykloneci was to fulfill what lay ahead for him in his life.

Controlling the weather was only an added bonus in this situation—the real input of this exercise was to be able to control the thinking and force the entire mind to be used in a very intense and focused way. Changing the storm tracks is useful to control the amount of rain and move it to the needed areas. But the primary focus of this entire exercise is how to use your entire mind to bring about what was needed and learning how to stay focused no matter what happened around you or to you.

This intense focus was a needed and necessary ingredient for anyone who wants to enter the battles for the king. This works to help them to stay focused on what is happen-

THE BEGINNINGS OF NYKLONECI

ing around them and to maintain their thinking processes no matter what happens. Thinking and focusing on what is happening around you and being able to maintain your thought processes is imperative if you are going to survive on the battlefield. Using this ability and learning how to focus on weather patterns was a relatively safe and positive use of this type of training, and it would show quickly how well Nykloneci was learning and what he understood about the whole process. This type of activity could be checked to see what kind of control and influence was being exerted, and it would help Nykloneci and Herbance to see the complete effect which was being placed on the storms that would come.

This ability brings with it an enormous responsibility to be accountable for what you do and how you change things. Most times it is only with the approval of the king that these changes can be made and followed through. Sometimes this ability can be displayed at the decision of the person who is trained in this kind of control. It is a great responsibility to learn how to do this, and it has to be used with great care.

The weather patterns can be controlled and manipulated by these people with amazing accuracy and can be used to control the work of the dark lords and their servants. Things that would normally be done in the wake of the storm could be stopped. This was effective in bringing the desires of the dark lords to a standstill, and they were powerless to complete what they wanted and desired to happen either in the storm or because of the storm. So Nykloneci began to work to control the storms that were forming over the large city where he now lived. He realized that this was harder than it appeared to be, and it took him a long time of practice before he was actually beginning to make any difference in the storm tracks.

But once he got the understanding of how it all works, he was able to focus his entire mind on what needed to happen. He began to have a minor impact on the storms.

It was at this time that Nykloneci's father and mother came for a visit to see him in the large city, and Herbance showed him more of what he needed to know and learn. Herbance was able to deliver another gift from King Hertfa during this visit—the ability for Nykloneci to begin to use his whole mind to apply himself in doing what needed to be done. King Hertfa had been gracious to the elder and given him a necessary ingredient that Nykloneci would need to advance and understand what was happening and why it happened.

Nykloneci did not realize that this gift was given to him at the time, but later he realized that something had changed within him, and his focus was greatly intensified. Nykloneci did not understand how this change had come about in his life. He only thought that it was normal for someone in the service of the king to advance quickly. Youth always feels like what is given is owed, and what is allowed is the proper thing to do. Little do they realize that many times this is not the case, it takes someone of standing to help them behind the scenes to get them to where they need to be.

After his parents left and went back to their own city, Nykloneci began to think that if this would work on the rain storms, then it surely would work on the large ominous storms that were of hurricane strength. This was his next challenge, to see what effect he could have on these super storms and figure out what he could do to try to change their course.

His first attempt proved to be more than he ever thought it could be. After a few hours of trying to get control over the storm, he ended up sitting in the corner of his bedroom whimpering and shivering from the amount of energy that he used to attempt this. It was at this point he determined that he would learn how to do this in time, no matter how long it took. Nykloneci was going to understand how to do this process and bring it to pass. He did realize through the gift of his sensing that there were many of the dark lords behind this storm.

This was the beginning of his understanding that things don't just happen, they are usually directed by some force that would bring about what it wanted to happen. This was the key to his growth and development and it helped him to understand that it was always a struggle between the king and the dark lords that made things in this world happen. Over time Nykloneci was actually able to begin to change the course of some of these storms, but it took many months of practice and vast amounts of his energy to bring even the tiniest change to the big storms.

This was an area where Nykloneci used lots of time and energy to work on his progress with controlling the weather patterns. He even began to understand how to stop the rain from falling when he needed to go out and do things. The stopping of the rain was an easy process after he had begun to grasp what it took to change the course of the storms. It was as easy as going out into the rain and holding his hand up and applying his thoughts to stop the rain from falling. Nykloneci was even able to cause the rain to return to the clouds which were carrying it and move it to another location after he did some practicing.

He was learning very quickly how this process worked, and he was able to apply it with great accuracy after a few months of diligent effort. Once he understood the impact and the implications of the storms, he was ready to begin to see what the battles were like, and it was time for him to meet the warriors of the king. With his new ability to focus his mind, the time spent on the battlefield would help him to understand how it all worked. His mind was focused, and his desire was strong, and with the gifts that King Hertfa had given to him—he was ready to face the warriors and learn from them.

The Warrior Training Begins

The first aspect of his training was for Nykloneci to be introduced to the warriors which he would be fighting with in the service of the king. This was a daunting task because many of the warriors would not willingly subject themselves to helping one so young and so inexperienced. The usual taunting began, and the mighty warriors of the king made sport of Nykloneci. This was normal for them to do to someone so young and inexperienced because most times when someone like this tried to learn, it was only a matter of time before they fell away and would not interact with the warriors anymore.

It seems that the young ones fall away quickly because of the draw of life for them. They lose themselves in their lives, and they stop serving the king until they get older. The warriors knew this was the normal pattern and because of this they usually avoided helping a young one to learn the art of battling.

They all knew that it was a waste of their time and talent to take the time necessary to show one so young how to fight because the end result was normally the same for all the young ones. They come thinking they are ready, but once they get into the thick of the battle, they lose heart and want to stop and leave and never return to the battlefield. Some even come to the battles with the preconceived notion that they should lead in the battles, and this is not allowed for the young ones. They lack the experience and expertise needed to lead, and many of them see what happens, and they feel slighted by not being allowed to have a major part in the battles. The young ones often leave upset and disgruntled with the whole battlefield experience.

Even knowing this, the elder attempted to move Nykloneci along in his training to gain the understanding that he would need. Herbance was hoping that Nykloneci would go forward and continue with this service to the king. The mighty warriors knew that this was the son of the elder, and they showed him more respect than they normally would have because of the years of service which the elder had given to the king. They all knew the past of the elder, and they also knew that the elder had never said no to the king with any request which had been made of him.

They respected and honored the elder because he had fought alongside of them for many years, and he had earned his place among them. The warriors all knew that the elder was shown a tremendous kindness by the king with allowing someone so young to enter with them into the battles that would ensue. So the teasing and prodding that came to Nykloneci was always tempered with who the elder was and the relationship that had been built by many years of serving together. Nykloneci was given chances that would have taken years for most people, within a few short months. He had no idea why, but he was thrilled that the warriors accepted him into their midst and allowed him to do things which were normally forbidden.

Most times it was mandatory for any new person to begin by assisting the warriors with whatever was needed at the bat-

THE BEGINNINGS OF NYKLONECI

tle sites. This could be anything from taking things from the battlefield for use at a later time to assisting the troops by bringing them what they needed during the battles. This process was how many of the warriors were able to gain what they needed for the next fight.

They would actually go onto the battlefield and gather the weapons and the materials that they needed to be ready for what came later in the next encounter. Every warrior was expected to gather what they knew they needed from the dead and dying, and this helped them to understand the seriousness of the battlefield. Nykloneci was only given this task for a relatively short time of only a few months instead of the years that this process normally took. It was a boost for Nykloneci because he was on the fast track to learning what he needed to know, and it allowed him to skip through some of the most important first steps.

The downfall to all of this is that it allowed the arrogance and pride which Nykloneci had within him from the effects of the dark lord, Lustureus, to also grow quickly over time. Nobody was looking for any effects like this to take place, so that is why they were missed and overlooked during his training period. This aspect of what was going on behind the scenes was the direct result of the involvement of the dark lord and would cause major problems later in life for Nykloneci.

Nykloneci moved along quickly and faster than most people could ever expect to gain their learning, and this was all due to the alliance which the elder had built up with the warriors over his many years of serving alongside of them. Nykloneci had no idea that what he was experiencing and going through was denied by the king in most cases. The king knew that the young ones would never be able to understand and stick with the process which needed to be done, but in this case special allowances were made because of Herbance.

Nykloneci was able to do things that most could only dream of in their wildest fantasies. He did not understand how this had all come to pass; he honestly thought that he had deserved what he was given. Nykloneci did not realize who his father was in his service to the king and would not accept it even if it were explained to him clearly. Nykloneci did not grasp that his father was one who had great influence and standing with the king and in some cases even advised the king on the best way to proceed in certain situations. This was all hidden from him, and it was done so he would gain humility and refrain from pride and arrogance in his service to the king.

The result of the training process was that one of the fiercest warriors in the service of the king took notice of Nykloneci. This warrior was named Gammy, he was a member of the royal guard of the king, and he was the one which most of the warriors would have nothing to do with; he was nicknamed the destroyer. This was a unique and interesting situation because this warrior was not known to like any new recruits very much, and he normally avoided them at all costs.

But something was different, this time he was willing to adopt Nykloneci and allow him to begin training with him on a personal level. Once again the elder had used his influence and asked that this be a possibility for Nykloneci. This was done so he would be able to get the best training possible and allow him to know all that he needed to learn from the best possible warrior available.

Nykloneci was adopted by Gammy and made his pet once he decided to follow through with what the king had commanded of him. Gammy would show affection to Nykloneci and allow him to get closer than anyone had ever gotten to him before. Gammy was the only choice to teach Nykloneci because he was the one who got things accomplished for the king, no matter what it took to get them done.

Gammy was also the most intense warrior of the king, he would realize what was needed and then respond before others even knew what needed to be done. Gammy would have been a leader among men, but most would not approach him because of his countenance and his immense size and strength. Gammy was one to be feared—and with good reason—even the warriors who served with him would often shy away from him because of his thinking and his actions.

This was an amazing feat in and of itself, for Gammy to teach anyone so young, and once the elder came upon this thought and asked the king, things moved forward quickly. Gammy allowed Nykloneci to accompany him to the battles and he would keep an eye on him while the fighting was going on. Whenever Nykloneci would get too close to the battle, Gammy would come charging his way and remove any of the warriors of the dark lords who got too close to him.

This strange alliance began quickly and grew with each passing day. The time came for Gammy to begin to teach Nykloneci how to fight, and he was an expert in every sense of the word. Gammy would toy with Nykloneci and allow him to spar with him. Gammy was always gentle with him and never damaged him with any kind of intensity. Gammy would often provide a quick smack or hit Nykloneci with the side of his sword to catch his attention. Gammy took the time to help Nykloneci learn how to defend himself in many different situations. This was not the normal or natural way that Gammy would treat the new recruits, but since the elder had requested his services, it went this way.

Gammy had known the elder for many years, and they had fought side-by-side for most of this time. Gammy was willing to honor the request of the elder about helping Nykloneci with his training. Even though Gammy would always instill fear in anyone that he put his attention on, he was a true friend and one who had the respect of the elder. Herbance and Gammy decided that it would be good if the elder acted as if he was fearful of Gammy. This would help to instill how special Gammy really was, and Nykloneci would understand that Gammy was a true warrior and one who everyone feared and avoided.

Once the elder had paved the way for Nykloneci, he was given opportunities that nobody had ever been given before by the king. This fast track with the gift of sensing made Nykloneci begin to feel like he was almost invincible. With Gammy's watchful eyes on him, it seemed this way to most anyone who was in the service of the king.

Nothing was able to get to Nykloneci to cause him pain or suffering when he was under the tutelage of Gammy. This relationship grew quickly, and the two of them were almost inseparable once the training began. Nykloneci was never told by Herbance about how things were able to progress so quickly. Nykloneci thought that he was earning his way, and in his own mind he felt like everything was going forward at the normal pace.

Little did he know that this fed the arrogance and pride which he had within him. This also fed his ego to the point where he began to think he was higher than anyone else in the king's service. Gammy protected him and allowed him

THE BEGINNINGS OF NYKLONECI

to learn his tactics, and his training grew over the weeks and months that followed. Nykloneci was learning from the best warrior and given every opportunity that was possible for him to get in his training.

Nykloneci was given the preferential treatment of a dignitary without him realizing it was because of his father that this opportunity was given to him. The king was against this opportunity until the elder agreed to be responsible for the actions of his son. Once this was put in place, the king gave Nykloneci a free hand to learn, grasp, and understand things which many other people were not privy to at this level of time and training.

Nykloneci began to learn and be a part of the warriors because of Gammy and what he was willing to do for him. Gammy had a new pet, and his name was Nykloneci. This brought many negative implications from the other warriors for a short time, and they avoided having much contact with Nykloneci for a while. But once they realized that his involvement was the result of the elder and his proposal to the king, things began to flow and move forward in a fluid motion, and things moved quickly.

Gammy treated Nykloneci much the same way as anyone would treat their favorite pet. Gammy would spend time with Nykloneci and pat his head and enjoy the times when they could be together without any kind of interference. Nykloneci did not grasp the magnitude of his standing, and this led to his feelings of being superior to anyone else.

These feelings did not go unnoticed by the dark lord, Lustureus, as he was constantly monitoring his progress. It seemed that nothing happened outside of his attention, and he kept close watch on the life of Nykloneci to see how he would develop and grow. Gammy became the constant companion of Nykloneci, and it was almost like the two of them became inseparable and had been in contact with each other for many years.

Many times when the king had special assignments for Gammy to carry out, Nykloneci was allowed to go along to learn and grasp what was needed for service to the king. This continued until the other warriors began to make sport of Nykloneci, and he became aware that this practice was happening.

When Nykloneci realized that his involvement with Gammy was bringing ridicule on him, he began to think of ways to get back at the other warriors. It was during this time that the dark lord, Lustureus, saw his opportunity to begin to plant the seeds of bitterness within Nykloneci. It almost seemed that any time something came out of his involvement with Gammy, the dark lord was able to use Nykloneci's feelings against him and cause him to begin to loathe the other warriors in this group of elite fighters.

Nykloneci made mental notes of the warriors who ridiculed him, and he kept these thoughts in his mind for the time when he could get his revenge on them. Instead of taking the times of sport as something which would always come, he used these times to begin to plot and scheme on ways to put the warriors that caused him problems in positions where they might be injured or destroyed. This was the direct result of his feelings of superiority, the fact that his ego had grown exponentially, and the constant and direct influence of Lustureus was always in the background of his life.

Nykloneci continued to learn from Gammy and started being able to handle a sword, shield, and staff with some efficiency. Gammy would be careful with him so that he would not damage him in any permanent way. The training continued with Gammy sparring with Nykloneci and allowing him to begin to feel like he may actually be able to prevail one day. Gammy took great pains to be sure Nykloneci was able to feel like he was advancing, and this was the direct result of his father's request to Gammy that he help his son. Even though this was not in his nature, and he did not like to play nursemaid to the new recruits, Gammy made an exception in this case. Gammy did all that was necessary for Nykloneci to learn what he needed to know to keep him alive in the battles. Gammy was willing to help Nykloneci because the elder had asked him to do this as a kindness to him. Their time together was good for them both, but as with most things too much of a good thing can often turn bad at just the wrong moment. Gammy continued to treat Nykloneci as his pet and his favorite sparring partner and this built the bond which was lasting and that would affect them both in dramatic ways in the future.

Gammy began to escort Nykloneci to the battles and show him what went on in them. Nykloneci was overwhelmed with how the battles unfolded, and he was especially interested in how the battle lines were drawn up before the actual battle began. Nykloneci could not understand why the warriors from both sides would line up and taunt each other before the battle started. It all seemed to be some type of game that they would stand and shout at each other and say they were going to prevail today and nothing would stand in their way.

Nykloneci did not realize or understand that most of those on the battlefield had been brothers in time past. But because of their different alliances, they were now on opposing sides of the battles. The shouting and the taunting were always a part of the ritual before the battles began. This activity served as a time for each to call to memory what they had done in the past and what they planned to do with each ensuing battle. Many times those who boasted the loudest were the first to fall in the battles as they raged on, but this was also part of the process.

When a warrior was wounded in the battles, they would be carried to the healers who stood off a short distance from the battlefields. Many were required to carry or assist those who were injured in the battles to their respective healers. This was an ongoing part of the battles and once someone was injured and fell, it was the job of those assigned to get to the fallen ones and assist them in every way possible so that they could get to the healers.

Once someone was injured, they would be ignored by the opposing forces most times, and they would be allowed to have someone to come and help them off the battlefield. At times the battles were so fierce that many would be destroyed in the conflict, and there was no healing for this situation when it happened. The bodies were left on the battlefield until the battle was over, and the winning side would be able to walk among the dead and gather their armaments and use them in the next battle.

After the time of gathering what was needed for the next conflict, the bodies would be piled together and burned as a ritual that would involve chanting about the deeds of the mighty and those who had fallen. At times, when this happened, if the person was someone of standing for King Hertfa, Scribe would be accompanied to the battlefield to read from their book so that all who were present would know who they

THE BEGINNINGS OF NYKLONECI

were and what they accomplished for the king. When this happened it would be a time of great sorrow, and many would mourn the loss of this great warrior of the king.

It was during this time that Gammy began to show Nykloneci that there were many portals available to use for traveling to distant places which would save time and energy to be able to carry out all of the missions for the king. Gammy took the time to show and explain to Nykloneci how to use the portals and how to identify them in places where most people would not see them or understand what they were for. The use of the portals was paramount in the training.

The portals would be an intricate link in the abilities of Nykloneci to advance and move forward in his service to King Hertfa. The portals were doorways which opened in every area of the world. Once anyone knew about the portals and how to access them, it would mean that they would be able to transport themselves through the portal and gain an advantage in any fighting circumstance. The portals were also used by the dark lords, along with the servants of King Hertfa. Portals could be used by both good and evil, and this was a way for the balance to be maintained between them. The portals could also be used to enter the different dimensional realms.

Gammy knew how to use the portals intimately, and he was very careful to avoid showing Nykloneci the dimensional portals. The only portals that Gammy showed Nykloneci how to access were the ones which would be used in battles; he did not show him the dimensional portals at this time in his training. This was done to gain the advantage which was needed on the battlefield so that he could remain alive and continue in his learning. Gammy knew the danger of the dimensional portals so he avoided allowing Nykloneci access to them for now—this would have to come later in his training; much later.

    The dimensional issue was one that Nykloneci did not grasp or understand at this point. Gammy knew that there were eleven different and distinct dimensions which could be accessed through the portals. Gammy knew that most of the activity between the forces of King Hertfa and the dark lords was kept locked away in the fifth dimension. This was done to keep the problems associated with the dark lords at a minimum for the king to deal with. They were only able to break free when a portal opened and allowed them to travel to the third dimension where most of the normal human activity was played out. But over time the dark lords had determined how to access the maze and travel through it in the fourth dimension. The only helpful benefit to this was the need to rest after traveling through the fourth dimensional realm before battles could be engaged. As time went by, it got easier and easier for the dark lords to access this avenue of portal use to the third dimension.

The Eleven Dimensional Realms

The first dimension is the place for the nonviolent beings. They refused to get involved with anything that went on between King Hertfa and the dark lords. Their input was that it was not happening in their realm so it did not affect them or draw their attention. These were the ones who kept to themselves, and if something did not affect them directly, they refused to become a part of anything that happened. These beings were left to themselves for the most part, and they did not want or desire for anything to change for them. If someone went to their realm, they would be ignored until they left. They refrain from any type of interaction with any beings from any other dimension. It is their belief and structure to maintain what they had and leave everything outside of their dimensional realm alone. These beings are far enough removed from what is happening in the fifth dimension that they accepted a non-interference position and they worked to maintain it.

This dimension was filled with crystals and everything looked as if it were created with crystals or made with crystals. The rocks in this dimension shone like the stars, everything has glitter and the feel of something radiant and alive to it. Most times when someone would travel to their dimension it was to gather the crystals and take them to their home dimension. Since these beings did not interact with most, it was a relatively easy process to go there and take what you wanted without any problems or issues arising from what you took. The crystals that formed in this dimension were both decorative and valuable, but the beings here did not seem to understand what value meant. They cared for their own and nothing was lacking for them in any way so they did not concern themselves with things of value.

The beings in the second dimension are more accepting of other beings. They are simple groups which are happy to be left alone. If someone travels to their dimension, they would welcome them and spend time with them. They have no desire to travel within the different dimensional realms; they are peaceful and would only join in war when they are threatened.

Whenever the portals would open in their dimension, they would place their animals in front of the portals and when this happened, anything that came through would encounter the animals first and leave quickly. Their animals are docile creatures which would not hurt anyone, but their appearance would often send anyone who came to their realm away thinking that it was filled with ferocious beasts. This was their safeguard, and they employed it any time a portal opened and for the most part, it was all that was needed to keep the beings from other dimensions from entering and staying long. These beings have an understanding of many things, and if they are questioned, they will answer with honesty and integrity. Their dimensional realm has the appearance of fields and meadows.

The trees in this dimension contain fruit and flower constantly so their realm is endowed with beauty. The climate in their realm would seem to be spring to those of us in the third dimension, always growing and blossoming trees and plants with fruit always available to anyone who wanted to travel there and engage the beings in this realm. The fact that they are willing to share what they have is another reason why many go to them. They have vast knowledge which they will share with anyone who takes the time to go and visit with them. They appear to be simple in their approach to life, but their learning and understanding is way beyond the appearance of life in their dimension.

The third dimension is the place where King Hertfa lives and carries out his duties as king. The beings in his dimension are humans with a desire to take what they want and form alliances with anyone that they feel could help them in their cause. The humans are creatures of habit and they are willing to meet anyone who came through the portals with what they presented to them.

If a raiding band came through from the fifth dimension, they would meet them with armament and force to try to push them back into the portal and return them to their own dimension. If someone came through a portal to their area peacefully looking for some information, they would warily question them and then decide if they would help them with their needed information.

Most times the humans appear to be brute beasts by most who came through the portals into their dimension. The third dimension is limiting to most beings and they know that the humans were difficult to deal with so most avoided them.

King Hertfa seems to be happiest in this dimension, and he is willing to be a leader for the humans because he knows that without his guidance and help, they would revert back to the beasts that they had been in their history. King Hertfa determined that it was his place to live among the humans and help them since they lacked many special abilities and he was willing to help them.

This dimension has a variety of climactic changes, some of it is desert, other parts are forest, and much of it is fields. This dimension also has many cities and places established for higher learning in life, but many in this dimensional realm are not open to the idea of the other dimensions. It is almost as if they feel like they are all that exists, and they are not open to the possibility that others may share their world, just in other dimensional realms. The inhabitants of this realm are often considered to be primitive in their beliefs and their actions. The constant wars which are carried on by its residents only furthers this belief and causes most beings to avoid them.

The humans in the third realm are considered greedy and unwilling to change in any dramatic way, they are locked into their patterns and don't adapt to change readily. Most of the beings from the other dimensional realms who come across the humans realize that their primitive lifestyles and warring factions are to be avoided until the time when they can advance and get past these dramatic issues. Humans are considered to be brute beasts in the dimensional realms and categorized as such within the teachings of the other realms.

The fourth dimension acts as a buffer zone between the third and fifth dimensions. It was created to be a place that would separate the two zones so the travel between them would be limited. It seems that over time it had broken down until it is not much of a problem for the beings from the fifth dimension to travel through it and go to the third.

The humans from the third dimension also learned to travel to the fifth through this dimension and over time it does not seem to be much of a barrier. The only saving part of the fourth dimension is that it is a dark and energy draining place which caused those who passed through it to need time to rest after the journey. The fourth dimension is a maze which is constantly changing so that it would not be easy for anyone to go from the fifth to the third and be energized to carry out what they planned to do. But this dimension has been used so much over time that its effectiveness has been lost, and it has become increasingly easy for anyone to move through it now. The darkness fills this dimensional realm and most of the features of this realm are still a mystery because of the constant darkness; so it is still unexplored as to its features even now.

The energy draining aspect of this dimension also keeps any exploration and research at a minimum for this realm. It seems most beings don't waste their time and energy on a place that is so draining and that remains in darkness so that it cannot be mapped and explored effectively.

There are beings that dwell in this realm, but they are rarely seen and most times they are not seen in the fourth dimension, but only when they venture out into the surrounding dimensions. These beings are known as the shadow people and they live in a dimension which will probably never be revealed to anyone.

Most people in the third dimension have seen these shadow beings, and they appear to be something that materializes in their realm out of a mist. It seems that humans are able to see them but only if they don't look directly at them. Many times they will appear and if the humans will only look at them out of the corner of their eyes, they will remain. But once the humans turn their full attention and focus on them, they will disappear instantly and will not return for them to view again. When the humans look at them indirectly, they will remain and often make gestures to them and even try to communicate with them. Very little is known about these shadow beings, and more time and energy will be needed to investigate them to truly understand what they are and how they travel to the other dimensional realms.

The fifth dimension is the place where most of the dark lords call home. This is also the place where most of the battles between King Hertfa, his faithful followers, the dark lords, and their followers take place. There were times when the fighting would spill over into the third dimension but for the most part the fiercest fighting took place here. Most of the third dimension battlers would travel through the fourth dimension to arrive at the fifth to join the battles that are raging. The fifth was reserved for those who had been faithful to the king in times past, but now they had decided to band together to try to overthrow the king. This is their realm, and once you entered into this dimension you are in the heat of the battles immediately. This is the place of almost constant battling, and once you enter this realm, you had better be prepared for what you would encounter. The fierce fighting which takes place here will leave you with a sense of the true understanding of how battles are fought. This also explains why you always enter this dimension with your weapons in hand and with the desire to totally destroy whatever you find.

The features of this realm are nonexistent for the most part, with all the battling going on it is pretty much a wasteland with not much vegetation or growth evident. The only thing dramatic in this dimensional realm is the appearance of the dinosaurs. It seems that this ancient dimension still holds these beasts even though they have disappeared from all the other realms. It is often wondered if somehow the battlers for evil are able to keep them alive and growing to serve some kind of purpose that they require. It is often rumored that the dark lords keep them as pets to help them to scare and motivate the people in the third dimensional realm.

It is also believed that keeping the dinosaurs has other ramifications, and that they may be used as food and clothing for the inhabitants of this dimension. Some of their dinosaurs have escaped from time to time and appear in the other dimensions but only in relatively small numbers, and they rarely have much impact when they are found. It is believed that the dinosaurs did not originate in the fifth dimension but were driven here by the efforts of the dark lords for some purpose that has still not been revealed. The fifth dimension is one of war, and anyone who travels to this dimension will encounter war that is unprecedented anywhere else in the other dimensional realms. The dark lords call this dimension home, and it is what they will fight to keep, even though there is nothing of evident value or food growth found here.

The sixth dimension is another place for mighty warriors who are ruthless and waiting for someone to be foolish enough to enter here. It seems that this one houses those who will battle anyone who enters their dimension. Their desire is only to kill and nothing else, they are the ones who will destroy whatever comes their way first and then wonder why they made the journey to them later. Nothing but death resides here, and there are few humans who will ever get the chance to pass through this dimension unscathed.

Most times it will take someone who is cloaked from their observance who will be able to pass through this dimension without suffering the wrath of these beings. They are ruthless warriors who live in the sixth dimension, but it is understandable that they react this way because the dark lords from the fifth dimension were accustomed to going there many years ago and ravaging their dimension. They realized early on that it was more beneficial for them to attack anything which came through the portals to them rather than wait to see how many of them would be destroyed for the pleasure of the dark lords.

The sixth dimension appears to be a desert wasteland, and it is a harsh and violent environment with almost constant sand storms. The wind never seems to stop blowing in this dimensional realm. There are no trees in this realm, and the water is hidden in various places. This is not a place to go visiting, and it proved to be a place where humans quickly learned to avoid whenever possible.

The sixth dimension has limited places for growing food, and these places are fiercely guarded and defended by the inhabitants. The warriors in this realm know for them to survive they must be willing to destroy whatever comes to them first in order to live for another day. Their past dealings with the dark lords have proven to them that they must fight first and then survey the damage after the battle is over. They realized that any innocents who were destroyed was better than waiting to see what kind of beings came into their realm. Time had shown them that their first requirement was to attack and destroy before they were attacked and destroyed by others.

The seventh dimension is a place that will be unlike any other place where you can travel in this world of King Hertfa. You would imagine that it would be a hostile place since it is next to the sixth dimension, but quite the opposite is true. Once you break free of the sixth dimension and get to the seventh, you would expect more of the same that you encountered in the sixth.

The seventh dimension is a place of almost perfect peace where you can go to rejuvenate and feel refreshed from all of what you had to endure to get to this place. It is a dimension of peace and beauty that is only rivaled by the third dimensional realm. There are places of sprawling meadows with flowers blooming and rivers flowing. There are trees which provide shade and produce fruit that is the loveliest thing you will ever taste and enjoy. The seventh realm is a place of quiet and one that literally takes your breath away. The beauty seems to go on forever, and the wind gently blows through the trees continually.

The only thing missing from this dimensional realm are the birds you will find in the third dimension. There is quietness in the seventh dimension that you will not experience in any other dimension. Many who have gone there describe it as the place to go before you get to heaven, a place of peaceful restful reflection and a place where you can truly think and not be bothered. Most who go to this dimensional realm want to stay forever; this is the lure and the desire of anyone who makes it this far. There is such peace that they never want to leave this dimension again, but alas any beings are always forced to leave it and return to their place in their own dimensional realm. The peace and quiet gets to where it is overpowering for any being who stays here too long and they have to return to their own dimensional realm.

It seems strange to think that peace will drive you away, but after a period of time in this dimension, you will feel the need to return to your own realm because of all the peace and quiet. This realm seemed to be reserved for short visits only, and there are no permanent inhabitants who stay in this realm. This realm is a place to come to for short periods of time to refresh and realize that places like this have to exist for the balance to be maintained within the whole dimensional realm. But you can only remain here for the time needed for the refreshing you need and then be ready to return to your own realm.

The absence of any permanent residents is a mystery which has never been solved. This dimensional realm seems ideal for some inhabitants, but it is rumored that a tribe of beings lived here long ago. They were invited to move to another place, and once they left no beings have ever been able to stay in this realm for long. This realm is only for temporary use—the peace of it seems to have the opposite effect from what you would normally associate with a place of peace. The peace seems to drive you back to your own realm once you have spent some time in it.

The eighth dimension is isolated—and for a very good reason. This dimension is home to the ones that would take over all of the dimensions for themselves, and they would take them by force and hold them hostage. The beings in this dimension are focused on dominion, and nothing can stand in their way once they determine that they will advance and take another dimension by force.

These are the ones who have been outcasts from their home dimension; they used to live in the ninth dimension, but they were counted as being too violent to stay in their home dimension. These are the beings, who have been cast out of their initial home dimension, and they only desire to take what they want—any way they can get it. These beings have no compassion, and their only desire is to dominate and destroy. They have the mistaken belief that they are the ones who will be left after everything in all the other dimensions is destroyed.

Their conquest is to be the only remaining beings who survive the wars that will be fought, and they have it in their minds that they will remain. They are by far the most ruthless beings that will ever be encountered, and they live to kill and destroy. They take by force what they desire, and this is probably why they are isolated in the eighth dimension.

The peace of the seventh dimension keeps them from entering and living there. The blessed peacefulness of the seventh dimensional realm keeps them in check, and they have often tried to invade this dimension only to be driven back by the peace which permeates this dimensional realm.

The trees in this dimension appear to be dead shells of what they once were. They were gathered in places and what used to be green and growing forests are now large areas of trees with no growth left. Skeletal remains were all that were left of the trees, branches that were long dead and reaching for the sky with no life left in them.

Anyone traveling to this realm will feel the oppression and the hatred which seems to exude from this dimension. The use of a cloak will be the only way for anyone to travel through this dimension unnoticed, and it will be a wise being who avoids this dimensional realm whenever possible. These beings are so hostile that they have not been studied to know what they do or how they live; their domination mentality keeps anyone from going to them for research or understanding.

The few beings who have attempted to go to this realm for peaceful study have never been found once they entered this realm. They have never returned after entering this realm, and it is widely believed that anyone who enters into this realm will be tortured and then eaten by the inhabitants. This belief has kept most from entering this dimensional realm because of the fear that accompanies such a belief.

The ninth dimension is the place of enlightenment. Those who live in this dimension are the ones who have learned how to be at peace and maintain what they have by the force of an enlightened will. Their understanding is so far advanced that they are not easily understood. They have evolved until they have the appearance of beings from another world.

They have gray bodies that are uniquely formed and they have no need of ears or any body hair. They do not communicate as the humans do with words. They have found that words can be destructive as well as instructive so they have stopped using words. They are so advanced in their living that they communicate by the power of their minds. They use telepathic utterance to converse with each other, and the first time you experience this you will be overwhelmed because it is such intense communication. They are able to place their thoughts in your mind with such force that it could destroy your mind.

Only those who are expert at using their minds can travel to this dimensional realm, an ordinary human would not be able to experience their kind of communication without being damaged. These beings are what most consider as the aliens that all humans think of with fear and trembling. These beings can travel through all the dimensional realms and when they do, they bring fear to all who come across their path. Their intense communication skills through the telepathy that they use can destroy the minds of most beings which they come into contact with.

THE BEGINNINGS OF NYKLONECI

Their advanced and intense knowledge is what has allowed them to realize the destructive power of the spoken word. This is why they have chosen to never speak again. Their utterances are always given in the mind without any words being spoken by them to protect them from what comes through the use of words.

Their dimension is one filled with beauty and flowering plants, which is believed to be their food supply. It has never been observed nor has anyone ever witnessed these beings eat. But the flowering plants are still thought to be the only viable nutritional objects available to them.

It is not known if these beings ever accept anyone from other dimensions. They quickly make it clear that they are not willing to put up with the incompetence from the beings in the other realms. The use of their minds has proven to be the only defensive mechanism that they use or need because it is so intense and destructive to the minds of the beings of the other dimensional realms.

Anyone who enters this realm is met with the most intense mind invasion by these beings that most stay clear of this realm after they happen upon it. A few beings are allowed to travel through this realm but only because they have shown the inhabitants that they are not coming to them to try to detract from their society.

Once you have experienced the inhabitants of this realm, you truly understand that whatever happened in their past has engrained within them the willingness to avoid the use of words. Most do not understand the power of their words, but this group of beings has come to understand that the use of words is far too dangerous to be allowed to continue for them.

The tenth dimensional realm appears to be the surface of the sun. The radiance and glory of the brightness in this realm makes most decide to stay clear of this place. What most beings do not know is this illusion was created so that most who came would turn back and not explore or invade this dimensional realm. The main portals are all facing this appearance of blazing and lifeless light and it was created by the beings that live in this dimension to protect them from outsiders coming to their place of habitation.

The tenth dimension is a place where what you fear would drive you away. Once you are able to get past the illusion of the surface of the sun and you pass this cleverly devised apparition, you are confronted by your worst fear. No matter what you feared, it would manifest before you to turn you back and make you leave this place.

The tenth dimension is strictly off limits to most humans and this is for good reason. Humans who come to the tenth realm are changed in their thinking and their approach to life.

The ones living in the tenth dimensional realm are keepers of the protected secrets of King Hertfa. This is their only application and they know that the secret things of King Hertfa must be maintained and protected at all costs. The beings in this dimension are the gods of old, the ones of renown who moved aside so that King Hertfa could become the king and master of the land.

These are the ones who gave their allegiance to King Hertfa and agreed that the knowledge of King Hertfa must be protected and maintained. These beings are winged creatures and they are the folklore of what creeps among the night in the third dimensional realm. They make trips to each dimensional realm to gather what King Hertfa deems as important, and they remove the things which some beings have found in their realm and taken back to their own dimensional realms.

These are the ones who come to you and cause you to shudder and feel the hair on the back of your neck stand at attention. Whenever they approach and come to you, the air becomes electric and you feel like you need to get out of the place where you are currently standing. They travel in pairs at the least, and groups of several at times to accomplish what King Hertfa commands them to do.

They appear as mist which settles in one place and then it breaks apart and moves with the set purpose to gather what King Hertfa deems important. These creatures are always cloaked, and only a few humans who have ever seen them will remember their features. These are the ones with the ability to demand attention and they will appear only for an instant to gather what they have been sent to collect for King Hertfa.

The legends say that these creatures are created ones which never die and they always accomplish what is needed for the king. They are shrouded in mystery, and when they come to anyone; their presence is always felt and marveled at by whoever they come into contact with. They never reveal themselves willingly, but once they arrive to do work for King Hertfa, they will do whatever he commands them to do.

These are the beings which nobody has ever befriended or become acquainted with; they reside to serve King Hertfa, and they are the faithful ones who do what he commands. There is a legend which says that if you follow them back to their dimension, you will be able to witness them in their true form and see them clearly. It goes on to state that those who have seen them will never desire to see them again. Once you have seen them in their true form in their own dimension you will be known to them forever.

These servants of King Hertfa are the faithful ones who work to uphold his authority and keep his secret things from falling into the hands of any of the beings in the other dimensional realms. Nothing escapes their notice and if they ever settle their gaze on you, you will be stricken with a fear of them that will never allow you to think of them without the fear coming to you.

It is stated that there is something about these beings in the tenth realm which can never be revealed, and if it is revealed, they will come and take you away by force to be with them until the time when King Hertfa calls your name in his throne room.

The eleventh dimensional realm is a mystery. The fact that most do now know of its existence and rarely will anyone travel to this realm helps to maintain it.

This realm is reserved in darkness, and it is rumored to house those who have fallen short of their service to King Hertfa. They are said to remain in this dimensional realm until the time of their end.

The only way to enter this realm is with a flaming staff, and few of these remain in service at this time. These rare items must be gained from the battlefield when the beings from the eighth dimensional realm break through and gain access into the fifth dimension. The rare times when this happens, many will be able to find the remains of the battles and use what they find on these beings as the extraordinary items of war.

These beings from the eight dimensional realm use all their knowledge and understanding to create items for war, and when they are given the chance to go to the fifth dimension they will take their items and try to conquer anyone who is present in this dimension. These are the ones bent on conquest, and they never attempt to gain peace with any beings they encounter.

The flaming staff from one of these is the only way to enter the eleventh dimensional realm, and when you enter extreme caution is required. The beings in this realm are reserved for the final judgment of King Hertfa, and they know that they fell far short of what he commanded them to do. These are the ones that live in agony and bondage which will never be revealed in the other ten realms. They were all given a chance to serve the king, and once they accepted this calling, they failed to carry out the desires of the king.

The beings reserved here are combinations of all the other ten dimensional realms and they are forever in darkness wailing and moaning because they know they have to wait for the king to decide when they will be judged. Their lot is to be in agony and misery until that great day arrives when King Hertfa will enter with his flaming staff and call them all to account for what they did.

They all know they deserve what is coming to them, but it does not extinguish their agony. These are the ones who willfully and rebelliously failed to carry out what was given to them to do by the king. They willfully disobeyed King Hertfa and their punishment is to remain in this eleventh dimensional realm until the time when he decides it is time to bring their suffering to an end.

This dimensional realm is the place reserved for those who were willfully disobedient to the king and he personally placed all of these beings in this realm by his own hand. Those who are placed in the eleventh dimensional realm will never escape it. When the king places them here, he binds them with chains that will never be removed until the time when they are judged.

These beings are the created ones. They are not born to other beings but created by King Hertfa, and they are only given one chance to serve him. If they fail, they are placed here until their end comes by King Hertfa himself, and they know that they had a wonderful chance to serve the king, and they failed.

The beings in this dimensional realm are unique in the fact that they only get one chance, and this one chance comes with devastating results if they fail. These are the ones who don't understand why they are only given one chance while many of the other beings in the dimensional realms of King Hertfa are given multiple chances to fail and then continue to serve. This great mystery will be revealed when King Hertfa enters this realm with his flaming staff and brings them out, one by one to judge them.

The Portal Knowledge

Nykloneci was to learn that there were many places one could go through the portals where no humans existed. Some of the dimensions contained strange beings with an appetite for fighting which was unmatched in Nykloneci's world. Once they found a portal and could transport themselves through it, they would appear and ravage anything that they came across.

This was what made the use of portals so dangerous. Many times when a portal was used, it would alert the beings in the dimension which was traveled to that one had opened and they would attempt to use it to gain access to another dimension. The portals that were opened would remain in service for a period of time, and many times the portal would stay open and useable for a few days to a few months.

Using the portals required that you kept track of which ones you had used, and if you went to a dimension where the savage invaders lived, you had to place a guard at the entrance of the portal to be sure that none of them came through undetected. The use of portals was to be limited, and you could only access them when it was needed, and they were not to be used for selfish gain or for pleasure travel.

Portal use was explained to Nykloneci as a way to gain an advantage in the battles that would come and to help in traveling to remote locations or other dimensions without expending time and energy to travel. Nykloneci was being given this preferential treatment because his father, the elder, had a great plan for him and it had to be carried out in a timely and intricate fashion.

The knowledge of the portals was given to Nykloneci because he would need their use to carry out his service to King Hertfa. The portals were an ingenious way to travel that did not take time or energy as it did for most things. The opening of the portals was an intricate part of serving the king, and it allowed things to be accomplished with extreme and intense accuracy.

Portals could be used to travel through the fifth dimension with the element of surprise on your behalf. Many times the battlers would travel to the fifth dimension unnoticed by the inhabitants of the fifth dimension and be engaging them in battles before they could take time to prepare and ready themselves for battle. This was the primary use of the portals, to advance the battlers to the battlefield without allowing the dark lords to see them assemble and move toward the battles. Once the battles were started, the smaller portals could be accessed to allow the battlers to move out of their ranks and travel behind the enemy to catch them with their guard down. This was an effective use of the portals and allowed the battlers to gain a distinct advantage in the heat of the warring that was going on.

The totality of the use of portals was not given to Nykloneci directly by Gammy. He knew that with this much knowledge and understanding, it would be dangerous for Nykloneci to grasp the whole concept of the portals in the early stages. Gammy knew that once Nykloneci began to use the portals, he would see that they could be used for more dramatic things than battles.

The portals were effective to travel throughout the eleven dimensional realms, and Gammy knew that in time Nykloneci would grasp the importance of their use. The portals could be used to open a place to travel into, and they could also be used to open a place for something else to travel to you.

King Hertfa had invented the portals as a way to travel to different places without the use of time and energy. The portals were his secret for many years, and it was his most effective way to travel throughout his land. He would simply open a portal, enter into it, and cause it to open in the place where he desired to go. This was a significant improvement over having to take the time to travel from one destination to another one where time would be a disadvantage to the king. He could instantly appear in one location and then within a moment of time he would leave and appear somewhere else.

After using the portals to travel throughout his land, the king decided that they would be useful for traveling between the dimensions. The dimensional issue was one that was clouded with problems, and it was often difficult to move through one dimension and travel through to the next one without being detected and causing great issues to be brought to pass.

The many warring factions in the different dimensions made it difficult and unsafe to use them to travel from one dimension to the next one, so King Hertfa applied his portal ability to use in the dimensional realms. This allowed his traveling to be unnoticed, and he could move from one dimension to the next one without being detected or noticed. This greatly increased his ability to maintain a presence in all the dimensions and maintain his place of power and authority without needing to secure effective places to maintain in each dimension.

His ability to travel through the dimensions using the portals made it almost impossible for anyone to detect his presence or to know where he was going to show up next. This aspect was pleasing to the king, and he incorporated the portals and their use to his close and loyal followers.

After several years of service to King Hertfa, the portals were explained to his followers, and they were then allowed to start using them. The only requirement was for his faithful followers to only use the portals with his blessings and knowledge. It was simple to inform the king of the need to use the portals and once this started happening with increased frequency, the king no longer required his faithful ones to inform him of their usage. King Hertfa trusted his servants to use the portals properly and allowed their use for the times of those in his service.

The portals were being used with increasing frequency, and this brought attention to those who used them. The dark lords began to understand that something was being used to allow the faithful ones of the king to travel around with incredible speed. This brought the attention on anyone who served King Hertfa with greater intensity by the dark lords until they gained the knowledge of the portals and how they were being used. After this happened, it was common for anyone to use the portals that were established, and it was hard to limit the usage once the dark lords began to access them.

King Hertfa knew this would eventually happen, but he hoped that it would be eons before the dark lords learned how to use the portals. This was not the case, and the dark lords

THE BEGINNINGS OF NYKLONECI

began to use the portals as much as King Hertfa and his faithful followers used them. Once this came to pass, the use of portals was limited by King Hertfa. The king would allow his servants to use them when it was utterly impossible for them to accomplish what he wanted done in any other way. Portal use was extremely limited during this time and the king was sorry that he created this way of travel because he knew the dark lords would use them to their advantage now.

Gammy instructed Nykloneci in the proper use of the portals according to the guidelines set in place by King Hertfa during the battles. This was paramount for him to begin to understand how to use them and gain the understanding of what advantage they presented during the battles. Gammy was careful to keep Nykloneci close, and he would only allow him to use the portals when the fighting became heavy and close to them. This was how the important ones could battle and get close to the enemy before they would access a portal to take them out of the intense fighting.

Once the dark lords gained this understanding, they used them the same way to escape the times when they would be attacked personally. During this time when the dark lords would access the portals, once you entered one, you never knew what you would encounter after you entered. At times you would come face-to-face with the enemies in the portals and this created intense times of wondering if you would survive. The use of the portals became dangerous once this happened, and it was only then that everyone who served the king knew their advantage had been compromised.

It was at this point that the balance of power and advantage was changed and would never be the same again. King Hertfa knew this day would come, and when it did, he realized that his control would be greatly diminished. But as with all things where a distinct advantage was held, the change was inevitable and would come at some point.

With the dark lords knowing the portal usage was now available to them, it created some problems that everyone knew would come sooner or later. Since the dark lords were also using the portals now, it was only with great care and understanding that anyone used the portals after this time.

Gammy was an expert at using the portals to travel within the battles and to use them to move through the dimensions. Even with this vast knowledge that he had about the use of the portals, he still was hesitant to explain to Nykloneci how to use the dimensional aspect of them. He knew that when the time was right the proper information would be given to Nykloneci, but for now he was content with showing him how to use the portals during the battles between the king and the dark lords. His primary focus was for Nykloneci to be able to understand how to stay focused and keep himself out of problem areas within the battles.

Once Nykloneci began to understand how to defend himself, it was time for him to do what he always hated to do. Nykloneci was not one to spend much time in a learning posture, and this part of his makeup was a direct result of his involvement with the dark lord, Lustureus. This connection was unnoticed by everyone; even Gammy did not seem to realize what was happening with Nykloneci's frequent mood swings and his feeling of superiority.

The learning parts were not the favorite part of the training for Nykloneci, most of this was just a waste of his time in his own mind. Nykloneci was a self appointed warrior, and he was ready to start battling and doing what was necessary to advance the purpose of King Hertfa. Taking time to learn new things did not enthuse him or help him to gain what he felt like he needed. So needless to say, Nykloneci did not like to have new things come to him which required him to take time to learn, he was much more interested in battling and gaining the advantage over the enemies of the king.

The Secrets of the King

The elder decided it was time for Nykloneci to meet with one of the king's special servants and one who would be able to show what he needed to learn in a way that would not seem like learning. The time came for Nykloneci to meet the person who kept all the records for the king. This was an unusual circumstance, and most of the people who were in service of the king were never allowed to spend much time with this person. Since he kept all the records for the king and wrote down all that happened in the realm of the king he was referred to as Scribe.

Scribe was a unique and outstanding servant of the king, and he was busy writing all the time. He had a deformity that the king recognized as being a unique and utterly amazing ability to allow him to do what was needed for King Hertfa. Scribe was different, and he did not realize or understand why most people were not allowed to spend time with him as he carried out his duties for the king. Scribe was born into existence with six arms and six hands—he was unique because of this malady, and it would have been a reason for him to be ostracized and removed from the company of most people.

But King Hertfa realized that since he needed someone with special abilities, and since Scribe has a desire to serve the king and he could use each set of arms independently, the king accepted him into his service as the keeper of the records.

Many cultures have worshipped Scribe because when he has to travel throughout the realm of the king to gather what is needed, they realize that he is truly a remarkable and unique being. Since most cannot explain what he is or how he is able to operate with his deformity, he has been worshipped by many as a truly divine entity.

His appearing throughout the realm of the king was so rare that many thought of him as a great being with much to do and this is why he rarely visited them. They also noticed that he was never alone when he visited them and this is why any statue or likeness that is made of him is always accompanied by other beings. Some cultures have even taken to portraying him as female with breasts that show his life giving quality and the breasts are shown to call attention to the others that accompanied him.

Scribe could carry on a conversation and continue to write with at least two sets of his arms while he talked about any subject that he was asked about. This amazing ability allowed Scribe to talk to someone and continue to write down the necessary information for the king. So his job as recorder of all the events in the lives of the people that the king deemed important was able to be accomplished by one person instead of a group of people trying to do the same thing.

Scribe was unique from anyone else in the kingdom, but the king allowed him to organize and facilitate the keeping of the records for the entire kingdom. Scribe did not seem to notice that his extra arms were a negative focus by many of the king's servants. He just gladly accepted what he was given to do and moved forward in keeping the records and being in charge of the library that housed the documents which he produced for the king.

Scribe was a one-of-a-kind individual, but he was humble and would gladly invite anyone into the library who was given the authorization by the king to visit. The king was always very careful to only let people go visit Scribe who needed information that was housed in this giant library.

Many of the documents that Scribe produced were of great importance and not available for many people to inspect or read. The king knew most of the work that Scribe did was top secret and would never be able to be viewed or used by most people. All the records about the lives of the king's servants were kept by Scribe, and he would write about their accomplishments in life and what they had done for the king.

Each person who served the king was given their own book so that all their accomplishments and exploits could be recorded and kept within the library. The elder knew that each person had their own book, and once they started in service to the king, everything they did was recorded by Scribe to be preserved for the king and his use.

King Hertfa was very careful to make sure that all the accomplishments of his servants were documented and kept in the library for future reference. Anything that anyone had done in their service to the king was recorded by Scribe and placed within the library in their individual book.

Scribe was also directed by King Hertfa to record events that happened in other books, so it was possible for what someone had done to appear in multiple volumes of the books that Scribe wrote. Many times references about the servants of the king would appear in many different books, according to how they performed their tasks for the king.

THE BEGINNINGS OF NYKLONECI

For example, it was possible for someone to battle for the king, and this event would be recorded within their own book. Reference to the servant would also be in a book that detailed what happened during a particular battle, and also in another book about the outcome of their service during the battle. Many times it would be possible to cross reference what someone had done for the king in many volumes that had been written by Scribe.

Herbance and King Hertfa decided that the only books which Nykloneci would not have free access to were the ones that had been written about Herbance. It would be better for Nykloneci to stay away from what Herbance had done for the king up to this point. King Hertfa determined that it would be better if Nykloneci did not know the intimate relationship that Herbance had been given with the king. At times it is easier for someone to form their opinions based on what they do not know instead of giving them information that they could not grasp or understand.

Herbance went to the king and requested that Nykloneci be allowed to go visit Scribe and begin to realize and understand the importance of seeing what was recorded. The king was firmly against this plan and stopped short of allowing Nykloneci to see what was kept in the giant library.

The elder had to explain why this was a necessary part of the training for his son, and once he told the king the entirety of his motivation and why it needed to be put in place, the king agreed.

The king was always willing to listen to the elder and would take his advice and advisement on many issues that came around in his kingdom. This only came about because of the elder's years of service and his willingness to do whatever the king asked of him. The king knew the desires and the level of service that he had provided over the years and this led to a special relationship between them.

The king was king, but many times when the elder would ask for something, the king would listen intently and then make his decision. Many times the king would make his decision, and then when he would inform the elder about what he had decided, the elder would make his case and explain why the king needed to rethink the matter. This would often lead to the king changing his mind and listening to the council and advice of the elder. Many times things that were set in place by the king were changed after their discussions.

The understanding of how to talk to the king had come over a long time of dealing directly with him. The elder knew that the king would often make decisions and implement them only to see the reactions of the people close to him. If the king knew what was going to be the outcome of his decrees, he would often make something very constricting for the people.

King Hertfa did this to see if anyone had the courage to come to him and speak to him about what he has decided to do. The king was honest and knew that many of the things that he put in place would be better served if someone would come to him and discuss the issue with him.

The elder had learned long ago how this all worked and whenever the king made a decision, he would often go and speak to him privately to see what changes could be made. The king loved these times of discussion, and many times it allowed him to see what the outcome would be by someone who had to deal with his changes.

THE BEGINNINGS OF NYKLONECI

The king always listened and would take the time to sit and ponder what decisions he had made, but only when someone would take the time to come and speak to him about them. The elder understood this approach, and many times the king would listen to him and then change his mind about some issue that he wanted to address and change.

King Hertfa was the ultimate authority—there was no question about this, but most times he was open to discussion about what he had decided to do. Many times the king did this only to see if anyone would challenge him on his decisions and once they did, he would listen intently and see if their arguments had any viable application.

King Hertfa was truly a compassionate and loving leader. He would take the time to listen to anyone who came to him, and many times he would wonder why more of his loyal subjects did not come to him about the decrees that he had made.

There were times when the king made what many would consider rash decisions, and he would hear about their discontent. But for the most part, the ones who complained the most never went to the king to air their grievances. This always baffled the king and made him wonder if they would ever come to him personally and discuss their issues with his decisions.

It was very important for Nykloneci to take the time to spend with Scribe and look at what was available in the library for him to see. Nykloneci did not realize it yet, but this was where the secrets of the king were hidden away from the world.

Within the confines of the library, there were areas that were strictly off limits to anyone except with the king's consent. Many of the documents housed within the library were filled with the king's battle plans and the items that he had commissioned some of his servants to make.

Many of these plans referred to the crafters of the king. Most people in the service to the king did not know or understand that the king employed crafters to make the items that he deemed necessary to be made. Most people thought that what the king had, with regard to his armaments and his weapons of war were acquired from other kings or taken during the battles.

The plans for all of the things commissioned by the king were housed in this library. It took special permission for someone to see what the king had in mind with regard to the items that he had commissioned to be made. The elder knew of this situation, and he also knew that Nykloneci had to be able to access these documents in order to prepare him for what lay ahead in his future.

Nykloneci was granted access to visit Scribe and to talk with him and ask him questions at first. He did not realize the wealth of knowledge and information that was kept stored away within this library. Nykloneci thought Scribe was busy writing all of the exploits of the warriors for the king. This intrigued him, and he wished for the day when his book would be started and written by Scribe.

Nykloneci had no idea the treasures that were within the walls of this giant library. The giant library housed all of the information about anyone who had ever served the king. At the very least, each person had a book of their own that contained this information about their lives, and many appeared in multiple volumes.

Everything that happened to them in life was recorded by the Scribe, and he kept a running record of all their accomplishments in life for the king. Anyone who did anything for the king had a book with the events of their lives recorded,

THE BEGINNINGS OF NYKLONECI

and as things happened, it was up to Scribe to keep track of the events and put them down in print.

Since Scribe had this unusual condition of having six arms, he was able to write nonstop, keep all of the facts straight, and record in each book what commenced with regard to serving the king. Scribe was able to carry on multiple conversations and answer questions while he continued to write in the books. This ability allowed him to be an invaluable aid to anyone that needed to learn what was needed to serve the king.

It was possible for Scribe to hold three different books in his hands and write in them all at the same time. This was quite a feat for anyone to maintain, but he seemed to be ideally suited to his task, and the king gave him control of the library.

With this control that Scribe had, it also gave him incredible insight and understanding about all of what the king determined and wanted to come to pass. Scribe knew all that King Hertfa had commissioned and all of the things which he desired to come to pass. This information made Scribe a tremendous asset to the king and a tremendous liability at the same time.

King Hertfa knew that Scribe could be a dangerous force to be reckoned with. Knowing that Scribe would do all he could to help the king bring to pass what he desired, it was imperative that safeguards be put in place to maintain what Scribe was able to do. King Hertfa understood what Scribe was capable of, and this led him to be very careful about how he managed and maintained Scribe in his position.

Scribe would welcome anyone who was sent by the king, and he was cordial and willing to discuss any subject that the king had given permission for the person to gain. The king was in almost constant contact with Scribe because it was essential that everything that was happening in his kingdom be recorded.

The king would come to Scribe and ask him if he was current on the main workers, and Scribe was always able to answer that question with a positive response. The king was pleased with Scribe and would allow him much latitude in his duties because he knew that Scribe would always maintain the archive that was being built in the library.

Since Scribe seldom left the library, he would do most of the writing himself, but on very rare occasions, Scribe would leave the library and travel throughout the kingdom. When he was allowed to leave the library, he would have assistants who would come and take over the writing of the records. This rarely happened, but it did while he went throughout the land gathering what he needed to know so that he could update all of the volumes for the people who served the king faithfully.

It was during these times of walking the land that Scribe was the most dangerous. Scribe was the one that the king had selected to bring about the end of his empire. Scribe knew that when he walked the land he was in danger of bringing about the end of the empire of the king.

So the king decided that anytime Scribe went to walk the land, he would always be accompanied by two of his most faithful warriors, members of the Royal Guard. These warriors were sent along with Scribe to protect him but also to make sure that Scribe did not gain what was needed to bring the empire to a swift and sure end before the king decided that this needed to be done.

It seems there was a parchment that would be read by Scribe when it was time to end the empire and bring all that the king had built up and maintained to a swift and sudden

THE BEGINNINGS OF NYKLONECI

end. Scribe knew that he was the one who was designated to bring this to pass, but he also knew that this was his ultimate purpose to perform for the king. Scribe knew what he was ordained to do and he knew and understood that when he gained access to this parchment, the empire of the king would end quickly and dramatically.

The two warriors of the Royal Guard were always sent with Scribe to be sure he did not gain access to the parchment before it was time and that the king could depend on them to maintain his kingdom. One of the warriors who always walked the land with Scribe was Gammy. The other warrior who was sent with Scribe when he went to walk the land was one of the other Royal Guard of the king.

The Royal Guard consisted of the warriors that the king had in his service since his empire and kingdom were established. The king knew these were his most loyal subjects and they had battled many years in his service, and he knew they would do all that was asked of them without questioning his motives or his desires.

So you can see why it was important that Nykloneci was attached to the king through Gammy. This relationship was established so that the king would know anything that was going on in the land through what Gammy knew when he made the treks with Scribe. Since Nykloneci was given access to Scribe and the library, it was of the utmost importance that Gammy was able to maintain control and an inside track of what Nykloneci was accessing through Scribe and the library.

The reason this was so important was because all of the secrets of the king were housed in the library. The secret things of the king were in a part of the library that were hidden but that could be accessed from within the walls of the library.

Since Nykloneci was going to be spending large amounts of time within the structure of the library, he might happen upon the secret things of the king. If he did, Scribe or Gammy would be required to report this to the king immediately.

The battle plans of the king were also housed within the library, and they detailed all that the king had established with regard to what parts of the kingdom were essential to his maintaining control and what parts had to be protected at all costs. Even though these battle plans were essential to the king being able to maintain his kingdom, they were of little value compared to the secret things that the king housed within the library.

The secret things would only be safe if nobody ever realized what they were and how they were used to maintain the king in his role as leader of the land. It was important that anyone who spent time in the library was watched to be sure that if they happened on the secret things, that they could be explained away and not given the preferential treatment which they deserved. Since Scribe was almost always in the library, he was given the task of making sure that nothing came out about the secret things, and if they were discovered by anyone, it was his responsibility to make sure that the secret things remained secret.

Nykloneci was shown favor by the king because of the request of the elder that his son be given the chance to learn all that was needed for him to advance in his service to the king. The king had many reservations about Nykloneci learning all that was going to be given to him.

As King Hertfa put it, it took people most of their lives to prove their value to him. To allow someone so young to access the information of the king would probably prove detrimen-

THE BEGINNINGS OF NYKLONECI

tal to what the king wanted to bring to pass. But even with his reservations, the king relented and allowed this opportunity to be placed on Nykloneci because of the service of the elder to him. The elder knew that the king was placing a vast amount of trust in him by allowing his son to learn what the king had in mind for his empire.

The elder wondered if his son would be up to the task that lay before him, but he also knew as the king knew; it would take this opportunity to see if the young ones could be trusted with the things of the empire. So it came to pass that Nykloneci was given access to things that many of the servants of the king were never allowed to see. Scribe allowed Nykloneci free access to most parts of the library and he even answered his questions about the king and what he was trying to accomplish through his leading of the people.

It seemed that very little had been withheld from Nykloneci, and he did not realize the magnitude of what he was given access to. Nykloneci did not understand the importance that was placed upon him and his learning within the great library. It was almost as if he was thinking that everyone who served the king was granted access to all the items that he was allowed to see. Scribe had been instructed by King Hertfa that everything would eventually be shown to Nykloneci, but it was his purpose and direction to give him answers. Nykloneci went to the library with trepidation at the start, he was not sure why he had to spend time in a place of old records, or so he thought.

It was an amazing feat that Nykloneci was able and willing to go into the library and research the things which he needed to learn. He hated to go to school and learn the elementary things that were needed for him to live. And yet here he was in the library under the tutelage of Scribe learning all that the king had established to bring his empire to the height which he had taken it to.

Gammy came to see Nykloneci from time to time, when he was free to go see him in the library, since he was still carrying out all that was required of him in his service to the king. When Gammy came to Nykloneci, it was often to take him to spar and learn how to handle himself in battle. This was a needed break for them both because the learning and instruction from Scribe and the drudgery of serving the king with the mundane things were weighing heavily on them both. Taking some time to spar and spending the time that they needed to spend together gave them both a break from the work which they were doing and it gave them some refreshment in their lives.

Nykloneci loved it when Gammy would pat his head and tell him that it was time to defend himself as if his life depended on it. Nykloneci knew that Gammy would protect him, even to the point of laying down his life for him. But he did not understand yet that Gammy had to give him the best education in warfare that he could with what was coming in his future.

So Nykloneci was able to interact with Scribe and learn what he needed to know so that his place in the empire would be assured. Nykloneci was able to look at many of the books in the library but not any of the ones about his father. Most of the people who find out about this library are only given access to their own book or the book that listed their accomplishments in certain battles, and maybe the books of someone else who was in their own family. Scribe was very intense in this directive of the king and would only allow anyone the chance to view what was relevant to them.

Since Nykloneci was given this preferential treatment by the king, he was allowed to view many of the books in the library, and it was in one of those books that he came across the crafters of the king. This truly intrigued Nykloneci and he wanted to know more about the crafters. A group of people who built and created all that the king needed and wanted was interesting, and Nykloneci needed to find out all he could about them.

The Crafters of the King

When Nykloneci came across the information about the crafters, he was intrigued and wanted to know more about them. He asked Scribe who they were and what they did. Scribe described how the crafters were given the task to create what was required for anyone who had a special need to serve the king.

Scribe explained that the crafters were a little known aspect of the kingdom. The only people who were ever allowed to enter into their area were those of great importance, such as the general of the king's army or the warriors who needed some item made for battle. Once Nykloneci became aware that this was a part of how the king was able to maintain control over his kingdom; he wanted to meet with the crafters and see what they had been working on. This was strictly forbidden for anyone to do, unless they had direct approval from the king. Scribe told Nykloneci that he would have to wait until he was able to talk this over with the king before any arrangement could be made for him to enter the workshop of the crafters.

Scribe was able to talk to the king, and the king stated that Nykloneci had no reason to talk to the crafters so this was denied. The seeds of knowledge were planted into Nykloneci, and he vowed that one day he would gain access to the craft-

THE BEGINNINGS OF NYKLONECI

ers, and then he would know what they did and how they performed their service to the king. This thought was always on his mind after he became aware of these servants of the king. He wondered what they did and how they were able to make what the king required for him to be able to maintain control of his empire.

Nykloneci returned to the books in the library and continued his education of becoming familiar with the great heroes of the king. All of the books contained the exploits of the great warriors and those who had served the king with integrity and dedication. Many of the books which he was given to read contained information that was not known to most of the servants of the king, it was as if he was given pieces of a large puzzle which he would have to put together to understand the workings of the empire. Nykloneci was being given all of the information that was available for him to understand how the kingdom worked and what kept the empire together under the control of the king.

Nykloneci kept thinking about the crafters and what they did. This was almost an obsession for him. He could not understand why the king would deny him access into this area when he had given him access into the library. This puzzled Nykloneci and he began to question why the king would give him some information about the crafters and not allow him to visit them.

Nykloneci began to wonder how the crafters came to be in the service of the king and the significance of what they did. He began to wonder how the crafters were beneficial to the king for him to maintain control over the empire. He began to read the books with the overview of how the crafters were able to serve the king and manufacture the items that each of the great warriors used in the battles.

This fact became glaringly apparent to him as he read each book which listed the battles that had transpired and how the victory was attained by use of some special item. It became clear to him as he realized that many of the great warriors were only those who could think about what they needed and then present their needs to the crafters and allow them to build what they had envisioned.

This was one major part of the bigger picture of how the generals were able to overcome tremendous odds in some of the battles that took place. They had items which were made to fit their specific needs and this is what helped them to overcome the enemies of the king with a relatively small number of battlers. This became clear to Nykloneci that it was not only the number of participants in the battle but it was also what they had at their disposal which helped to sway the tide of the battle.

Nykloneci was quick to grasp that the king allowed the generals who served him faithfully to have almost unlimited access to the crafters. This information only made him desire to go and see them more and he would often stop and think of the time when he would get to meet them.

Gammy continued to come to the library a couple of times each week to take Nykloneci out to spar and develop his skills as a warrior. It was after Nykloneci became aware of the crafters that he had more questions about how the battles were strategized. Gammy was able to explain to him that it was not only who fought, it was how the battle was arranged and what items were used to stem the flow of the enemy.

THE BEGINNINGS OF NYKLONECI

Gammy was able to help Nykloneci understand that the battles had raged for many years. It was only in the last few decades that strategy was incorporated along with items which were being made to meet the needs of those who were leading the army of the king as his general. The crafters had become a major component in the advantage of the king's warriors.

When the crafters built what was requested of them, the battles could be fought with fewer participants and it was handled more efficiently. So this allowed more of the king's warriors to move about the king's territory without the need for all of his forces to be maintained within a small area.

This changed the way the battling was done; it used to be each side lined up on the battlefield and then they would charge into the opposing side and try to destroy as many as they could with their swords and axes. Now it was possible for the battlers of the king to advance on the enemy with fewer participants, and once they incorporated the items that the crafters had made, the battle was over quickly. Battles which used to last for days or weeks could now be accomplished within hours.

Nykloneci began to wonder why it took so long for the generals of the army of the king to understand the significance of the crafters. He made it his mission that one day he would get to go to the crafters and spend time with them and help them to see what was needed to circumvent the movement of the enemy with the vast array of things which he had in mind.

Once his imagination started, and it was still under some control by Lustureus, he could envision all kinds of things which could be made to change the tide of the battles and bring great victories for the king. Nykloneci now knew that he wanted to become a crafter for the king and help to make what was needed by the generals of the king. He began to think of how he could get access to the crafters and began to try to devise a plan that would allow him to become one of them.

Nykloneci decided that being a crafter for the king would be the ultimate position for him, and he began to try to figure out a way for him to fulfill this thought in his mind. This became an overwhelming obsession for him, and he tried to figure out a way that he could get to see the crafters. Nykloneci knew once he was given access to the crafters, he would be able to get so much accomplished for the king. He started asking Scribe how long it would be before he was able to see the crafters and meet them.

Scribe went to the king about this issue again and asked him if it would be possible for Nykloneci to meet the crafters and see the type of work they were doing. King Hertfa thought it over and again he determined that Nykloneci was not ready to view the work of the crafters. Scribe returned to Nykloneci with the bad news from the king and explained that maybe in the future he would get to meet the crafters but for now he needed to continue his learning in the library.

This answer came hard for Nykloneci; he began to understand that he was not going to be able to see the crafters or meet them. He felt like King Hertfa was withholding this from him, and he began to try to figure out a reason which would stand so that he could meet the crafters and find his place in the king's service.

When Gammy came to spar the next time, Nykloneci began to question him about the crafters and why they were such a hidden factor in the whole scheme of the king. Gammy explained that it was not a common practice for the king to allow anyone to spend time with the crafters unless they had a need which they alone could fulfill. Only a person of standing with the king was able to go to the crafters' room and spend time with them. The only reason for this was so that they could explain what was needed so it could be creatively made by the crafters.

Nykloneci asked Gammy if he was able to spend time with the crafters. Gammy assured him that if he was able to see them and understand what they did and how they did it, it would go a long way in his education for serving the king. Gammy laughed and explained to Nykloneci that he was only given time with the crafters when they needed to make something that he needed for the battles.

This spawned an idea for Nykloneci and he began to tell Gammy that it was time for him to get some new things made which would assist him in the battles. Nykloneci was hoping that if he was able to come up with things which Gammy needed, he may get the opportunity to go to the crafters with him. The idea of the crafters became such an obsession to the point where Nykloneci felt that if he did not get to see them and interact with them, he was not fulfilling his purpose to the king.

The drive to get to the crafters was not normal or his own desire; Lustureus was at work in this situation. Lustureus knew that once he was able to get Nykloneci to be involved with the crafters and learn their secrets of how they created what was needed, he would have the upper hand in his fight against King Hertfa. Lustureus knew if Nykloneci was given permission to visit the crafters, he would have another piece of the puzzle that he needed to defeat the king. This desire to get to the crafters was a driving force for Nykloneci now, and he knew somehow that one way or the other he would get to them.

Herbance went to the king to see how the progress was going with Nykloneci and to see if King Hertfa was happy with his training. King Hertfa expressed his concern about how driven Nykloneci seemed to be with wanting to visit the crafters.

Herbance remembered the first time he had entered the room where the crafters worked to create what King Hertfa and his faithful followers needed. This room was shrouded in mystery; there were whisperings about a famed room where servants of the king toiled to make the things that King Hertfa ordered for his warriors and generals. Most thought of this place as only a myth. They did not realize it could be real and a vibrant part of the planning for the battles which had been fought over the years. There was often a hushed mentioning of a glorious room where workers toiled to create items for the battlers of the king, but most did not give much time or attention to such talk.

The king had his secrets, and everyone knew that most of what went on within the throne room of the king would never be revealed. Most of his subjects did not involve themselves in the battles directly, so for the most part they did not concern themselves with a place where armaments and items of war and destruction were created.

Herbance remembered the first visit that he was able to make to this place where the crafters worked. This area was devoted to those who had the ability to listen to what was told to them and then have them make what was needed to fulfill the purpose they were given for building the armaments which were needed on the battlefield. All that was needed for them to produce the needed item was for someone to explain to them what was needed in a way that they could envision the item. Once this occurred, they would create it exactly the way it was explained to them.

What impressed Herbance most was the jovial attitude of the workers and how they were willing to work side-by-side with each one pitching in and doing what their part was to bring to pass what the king had ordered. The diversity of the workers was something which was not seen, they were of various heights and builds, it seemed like each person was perfectly fitted to do what their part was in the creating process. There were tiny people who could crawl under the smallest items and perform what they needed to do. There were giants who could lift enormous weights and place them delicately where they needed to be for their part of the work.

The room was circular and the ceiling was high with various chains and pulleys hanging in place to be used for different applications for what needed to be made. The windows were high on the walls, and it seemed the light permeated the building from every angle all of the time.

The large circular table in the middle of the room was perfect for work that needed to be done, as one craftsman finished his part, he only needed to rotate the table to the next person who worked to perform their task and allow the work to move forward. The large table was always filled with vast and different items that were being fabricated by these workers. Each one knew their location around the large round table, and they never squabbled or complained about what they had to do. It was almost as if the working was a perfect harmonious occurrence which moved forward with tremendous accuracy.

Such diversity all working together in a mission of completing all that King Hertfa and his generals desired to advance his empire. The efficiency that prevailed in this large room was unparalleled in the land. There was no bickering or arguing about how important one person's work was over another one. They accomplished what was assigned to them and moved along with undivided attention.

The work which was done around the large circular table was impressive, to say the least, but what was incredible was that each person knew what they had to do with infinite precision. It was almost as if they were communicating with each other without saying a word. It was only after Herbance got past the large circular table that he realized how each part which was being manufactured had intricate and complete plans laid out on a large rectangular bench toward the back of the room.

The circular effect of the room made Herbance think the room was only a large circular building, but once you got to the back of the room you realized that it ended in a large opening which led to another large room. This room was where all of the items that had been made were stored until they could be picked up by the person who had ordered them. The back of the room also had a doorway which was always closed. This seemed odd to Herbance, and when he questioned one of the workers about it, he was told that this door was always kept shut to keep what was housed in this room locked away. Herbance asked what needed to be locked away, and he was told this room was the place for all of the things which had been ordered and made that did not work properly or had never been picked up by the person who ordered them.

THE BEGINNINGS OF NYKLONECI

The items in this room were kept so that nothing would be lost, and the items could be referenced later if the need for something similar was required. There were three workers who catalogued and maintained the records for all the items that had been made by the crafters, and nothing was ever wasted. If something did not work, it was placed in this room and kept so that if possible it could be used again later when the need arose for it or something similar.

The crafters had things that did not perform as they were intended to, and with them always being needed to fabricate more items, the old ones were kept so that mistakes would not be repeated. The one thing each of the crafters was extremely proud of was that they could and would assemble anything which was asked for in the most efficient manner possible. Each one knew their place, and they all worked together like a finely tuned instrument.

The first thing that impressed Herbance about the work going on was it reminded him of a hive of bees, each one performing their task as needed and then moving on to the next thing without causing any problems for the rest of the workers. If anything did not seem to work properly, the ones closest to the item would take the time to see what had been done wrong, and they would correct the problem without placing blame. At times it seemed that each of the craftsmen could be placed in any position, and they would be able to fulfill what was needed and the item would be constructed properly and tested to be sure it worked.

The reason for his first visit to the crafters was when King Hertfa had granted for Herbance to have his first custom sword made by these craftsmen for his service. This was a tremendous gift that the king gave to Herbance; the crafters had to measure him to make sure the sword would be ideally suited for his needs. The handle was custom crafted with an insignia on it that promoted the king's future desires and his acceptance of Herbance. It was a wonderful time for Herbance to go to the crafters and watch them make his sword from beginning to end.

Shortly after this, the king expressed a desire for the crafters to make a shield for the elder, another precious gift that King Hertfa had bestowed on Herbance. The king had allowed Herbance to visit the crafters on several occasions, and it was not uncommon for them to see him from time to time to see what new items were being fabricated by the craftsmen. Herbance had truly gained the trust and admiration of the king and the crafters. He was honored by them all and given the freedom to input his ideas to the crafters for future use.

The crafters even made a staff for the elder and it was personalized by them for his use alone. Nobody else could use his staff to perform what was needed in the battles. This magnificent staff was instilled with a tremendous feature that allowed it to spew forth fire or ice as the need arose during the times of battling. King Hertfa was open to anything the elder mentioned to him about new items which he needed for the battles between the king's forces and the dark lords.

Herbance knew once Nykloneci was given access to the crafters; he would come up with a multitude of things that could be made to help the king and his servants in the battles which would ensue. Herbance knew that once this was accomplished and put in place, many new things would be created by the crafters for the king and his advancement. Herbance also knew that once this decision was made and Nykloneci would be given the chance to see the crafters and interact with them, things would change dramatically.

Herbance stood before King Hertfa and asked when it would be possible for Nykloneci to visit with the crafters and begin to understand how they worked and what they did. King Hertfa was against the idea and stated that this would be too much for him to allow. Nobody had ever been allowed to visit with the crafters unless they had a need for something to be made for the battles. King Hertfa knew that once Nykloneci was allowed to see the crafters, things would change quickly and dramatically so he again denied Nykloneci access to the crafters.

It was from this point forward that Nykloneci viewed the books in the library with the express intent to find out all he could about the crafters. Each new book that he was given by Scribe would be scoured over with the desire to find out more about this elite secret group who worked for the king to build and fabricate whatever was needed. Many of the books that Nykloneci read made mention or reference to the craftsman, but none gave a detailed description of them or what the room looked like. It was almost as if Nykloneci had the crafters in his sight, and he would not rest until he was given access to them.

This driving force was not his alone; Lustureus was also at work behind the scenes. Lustureus knew that once Nykloneci was given access to the crafters, things would change dramatically in his favor so he continued to cause Nykloneci to seek for a way to see the crafters. So the driving force became more and more intense as Nykloneci scrutinized the books that he was given more access to in the library. He was sure that one would have a detailed description of the crafters or at least give him some idea about how they worked and what they did for King Hertfa.

Reading the books became easier for Nykloneci now since he had a mission and one that he knew would come to pass one day. Meeting with the crafters became the most important driving force that would ever come to pass for Nykloneci. He even began to envision himself working among them, doing his part of the work to accomplish what was needed for the warriors and generals of the king. Nykloneci would often read something in one of the books in the library that would spark this kind of thinking, and then he would sit for hours trying to imagine what it would be like to work with the crafters, side-by-side.

The time spent with Scribe fulfilled a great many requirements that he needed to do in order to serve the king. Nykloneci began to see how the generals from the past had faithfully served the king, and once they had proven themselves, nothing was held back from them. He liked that King Hertfa was so easy to impress, and once someone was given his favor, nothing seemed to be impossible for them to accomplish.

Nykloneci read about the great ones of old who had carried the cause of the king across the land. He began to understand that serving the king was paramount in their lives and once they started their time of service, it was only a matter of time before the invitation was given for them to come and stay with the king. All of the faithful servants of the king who attained to greatness by becoming the generals of the king were handsomely rewarded for their service. Nykloneci knew that one day he would be able to become a crafter for the king, and he waited impatiently for his time to come.

The King's Son

During his time in the library, Nykloneci came across several references to the king's son. This intrigued him, and he decided that he needed to meet him one day and talk to him about how the king managed his empire. After he had this thought in his mind, it became clear to Nykloneci that he did not know who the son of the king was or what he looked like.

He questioned Scribe about the son of the king, and Scribe laughed out loud and asked him why he was interested in him. Nykloneci explained to Scribe that since the king had a son and he was the son of an elder, it might be a good idea for them to sit and talk sometime. Scribe asked Nykloneci when he wanted to accomplish this goal in his life. Nykloneci said that someday soon would be good. All of his learning and understanding that he had gained through the use of the library would prove useful to this discussion which he hoped to have.

Scribe pointed across the library and asked Nykloneci why he was waiting. The son of the king was in the library most days, and he was here now. This shocked Nykloneci, and he looked over and saw the person who Scribe had pointed at, and he wondered who he was. This person had been in the library almost every day while Nykloneci had been studying and learning. Now he felt foolish and realized the king's son had probably heard him make reference about him to Scribe. Nykloneci wondered what he should do and if it were possible for him to meet with the king's son and talk to him.

Nykloneci suddenly realized how foolish he had been to mention to Scribe that he wanted to talk to the son of the king. He looked up and there before him stood Susthris smiling at him. Nykloneci did not know what to say or what to do next. Nykloneci stood up and started to bow to Susthris when he reached out his hand to him and asked him, *what do you want to talk with me about?*

Nykloneci stood speechless, not knowing what to say or do next. Susthris smiled at him and said, *it is ok, I have seen you in the library many days and I wondered what you were searching for in the books that you were reading.* Nykloneci expressed how it was determined by his father, an elder that he needed to spend time in the library and understand how people had served the king. Susthris smiled and said, *yes, I know him well, and he has served my father faithfully for many years now.* Nykloneci did not know what to say or do next, so he just stood there waiting to see what he would be asked next. Susthris asked Nykloneci to sit and talk for a while since he had the time to spend with him and answer his questions.

The first thing Nykloneci wanted to ask Susthris was how it felt to be the son of the king and what people expected from him because of his position. Susthris smiled and then laughed at this question, and then he looked at Nykloneci and said *most people think being the son of the king means that I have to do certain things or act a certain way, but this is not true. I am my own person and I have my own things which I enjoy and work to accomplish in my life. I do support the king and follow what he asks me to do, but not because I am his son but because it is the right thing for me to do. Being the son of the king does not make me special or important in any way it only shows my affiliation to him by being his son.* Susthris made it clear to Nykloneci that he was his own person and he should not try to do what people expect of him but to do what he knows is right for his life. This was not the kind of ideals Nykloneci expected to hear from the son of the king, but it did make very good sense to him. Susthris explained that so many people think the son of the king is a carbon copy of the king and this is not the case at all. Each subject in the kingdom should be their own person and this applies to the son of the king as well as to any other person.

Nykloneci determined to take a bold step at this point and ask Susthris about the crafters. Susthris explained that this was information that was only known to those who needed their services. One day when Nykloneci was in a position to need them to make something special for him, he would be allowed to go and meet them. Nykloneci explained that he wanted to be a crafter for the king and Susthris laughed again. Susthris had to explain the crafters were very special and secretive people, you could not just decide to become one of them. He further explained that it took great ability to become a crafter for the king and not many were qualified to do this important part for the king.

Crafters were selected by the king, and he would only do this when it became necessary for someone to replace one of the crafters who do this work because they were no longer able to perform their duties. Whenever this happened, and it did not happen often, the king would travel throughout the land and see the work of those who were already in some trade of building things. These were the ones who were considered to fill a place within the crafters and only after observing how they work alone and how well they were able to work with others. This answer did not sit well with Nykloneci, and he thought it was a very limiting way that the king chose to fill the places needed within the crafters. He still did not understand that some are born to do this and some are born to do other things—you don't always get to choose what you need to fulfill, you just know it and work to accomplish what is needed.

Nykloneci felt like he was again being denied what he wanted to do and accomplish for the king, and now he was even being told this by the king's son. Nykloneci began to realize that what he wanted may never come to pass, and this frustrated and upset him. Here he was talking to the one person who he felt would be able to understand his situation, and all he was hearing was that he needed to be his own person and do what was right.

Nykloneci wanted to understand why the king's son would tell him this so he asked him again, *what do you do to support the work and empire of your father the king?* Susthris looked surprised, but he still answered the question. He stated he was the king's son and it was required that he support the major issues of his father. He also added that most of what his father was doing was right and just, so this was not an issue for him; it made it easier to follow the command and directives of his father.

Susthris also explained to Nykloneci many people naturally thought that he would, in time, take over for his father. But as far as he was concerned, this may never happen. He did not live his life as if he was preparing to take over being king. It was much easier and better for him to do what he felt was necessary to support his father and not worry about anything else. Why should he plan to do something that may never happen? It was much better to be his own person and follow what life gave to him and not try to plan and figure out what to do later in life, which would all come later. Susthris explained to Nykloneci that he needed to figure out what he wanted to do to serve the king. It was beneficial to listen to others and this would be good counsel, but the end result was that Nykloneci had to decide for himself what he wanted to do and how he would serve the king with his life.

It was at this point Susthris stated that Nykloneci would never be an elder to the king like his father. This was not a natural progression in life, and he should not feel or think this way. He explained that because of the experiences of Herbance and his willingness to serve the king with his whole life, he was given treatment which most would never gain.

Nykloneci looked at Susthris and asked him, *what do you know about my father and his service to the king?* Nykloneci also asked *how far does this service go and why would the king show him such favor when he does not deserve it?* Susthris explained that he could not go into this area now but maybe in the future he would be able to talk to Nykloneci about it in depth. For now all he could say was that nobody deserved what they got from the king, most things were free gifts from the king and only to those who proved they could be trusted. Susthris told Nykloneci that he came to the library to see what had been done by the mighty servants of the king. He explained that most people were not worthy of what the king gave them, but this was his way and what he did.

Nykloneci was shocked with this information and asked Susthris what he meant by his statement. Susthris explained most of the people who serve the king only do so with limits in place for their service. Most would only do so much for the king and only when it was absolutely necessary. He went further and told Nykloneci about many who served poorly as general and did not accomplish much of anything for his father. But at the time they were the best choice that the king had to place them in this position of leadership. Nykloneci did not understand this and asked how this could be. Susthris explained, *not all the people in the empire are faithful servants of my father, many serve the dark lords and do all they could to try to destroy my father the king.* Susthris also explained, *sometimes the best candidates to be general would not accept the position, and this caused others who were not as qualified to be placed as general.*

King Hertfa knew they were not what he needed, but it was imperative that he have a general for his army, and his own troops would fill in the best they could for those generals who did not do the job well. Some were willing to serve, but they could not do the job so the army of the king suffered and many battles were lost in times past because of the generals. During this time King Hertfa decided that if he did not have the proper people in positions who would support his reign, he would need something to tip the scales so that the balance could be restored.

It was during this time that he implemented the crafters and allowed them to begin to create items that would help those without the natural ability to lead so they could still advance and move his empire forward. This is why the crafters have been kept a secret from most of his loyal subjects until a time when he knew he could trust them to assist and help with the battles. Only those with a direct need were allowed to visit the crafters to help them understand what they needed so that their items could be manufactured correctly.

THE BEGINNINGS OF NYKLONECI

Once this began to work and the king saw how well these people worked together to serve him and build the items which were requested, he implemented that the crafters could only be visited by those who needed items made. This edict is still in force today and will remain; nobody outside the area of battling will ever go to the crafters because they are too valuable to the king. The king will not allow anyone access to the crafters until they show him a need for something new that they can make to help the king maintain control of his empire.

After Susthris explained the reasoning why not just anyone could go to the crafters and see what they were working on, Nykloneci understood how important this group really was. For some reason he did not understand that the crafters were the stopgap for the king. They truly were the ones who helped the king to maintain control through what they fabricated.

This helped Nykloneci to understand why the king kept denying him access to the crafters and answered more of the other questions which Nykloneci had. With this explanation of how things were working and the willful admittance of Susthris that many of the generals were not effective or the right person for the job, this helped him to understand why the tide of power seemed to ebb and flow at different times for the king.

Nykloneci now understood that the crafters were the ones who really helped the king to maintain his control and position more than any general had for several years. The king was protecting the best resources that he had and denying access kept the crafters from focusing on people visiting and kept them occupied with building and fabricating the items which were needed to help in the battles with the enemies of the king.

Nykloneci asked Susthris about Scribe next. With gaining this understanding about the crafters and what they meant to the empire, he now knew that their work was more important than most realized. Nykloneci asked why Scribe had to be locked away in the giant library all the time and why he was not allowed to travel throughout the empire to gather the information that he needed to record for the king.

Susthris called Scribe over and told him that he was able to explain to Nykloneci why he spent so much time in the library. Scribe started his answer with the fact this was his job and his service to the king. Susthris smiled and told Scribe to explain the reason why he stayed in the library, and not the answer that he had rehearsed for the few people who came to the library from time to time.

Scribe put down the books that he was holding and sat down with them and looked at Nykloneci and said, *I am the key to the end of all that the king fights to maintain.*

Nykloneci laughed and looked at Scribe to see what silly thing he might say next. When he looked at Scribe and saw the look on his face, he understood that there was nothing silly or comical about the statement which Scribe had made. Nykloneci asked how Scribe could be a key and what lock was he to be used for. It was time for Scribe to smile and look at Nykloneci with a grin on his face that showed he knew Nykloneci had no idea who he was or what he was assigned to do.

Scribe laughed and then looked at Susthris and waited to see his reaction, but he was already laughing, too. Scribe said, *I am not a key that fits into a lock as you might think or suppose. I am the one who will start the end of the empire for the king.*

THE BEGINNINGS OF NYKLONECI

Nykloneci was totally confused now, how could the king allow someone who would bring an end to his rule and his empire to serve as only a trusted and loyal servant? Nykloneci looked at Scribe and asked how long he had been a captive of the king and what hold did he have over him to keep him locked away in the library.

Scribe looked at Susthris and smiled at Nykloneci and stated, *I am not a captive of the king.* He told Nykloneci *I am a very close and dear friend and supporter of the king.* He further stated *the king has given me instructions about how his empire will come to an end and he gave me specific details about how it will all happen.* Scribe told Nykloneci, *I am the one who the king has chosen to start the end of the empire. It is my job and duty to follow the instructions of the king to the letter and do what the king has asked me to do when things come together.* Nykloneci sat there wondering how could this be? How could someone who records things for the king actually be the person who will bring the empire to a close? Scribe waited a few moments before he continued his discourse on what his part was in bringing the empire to an end.

He explained, *there is a parchment which was hidden long ago and when the king determines it is time, I am to go to this secret place and get the parchment and read it. Once I do this, the beginning of the end will take place and many strange and marvelous things will happen when I read this parchment.* Nykloneci again thought he was being made the fool in this conversation and he started laughing and looking at Susthris waiting to see what he would do. Susthris looked at Nykloneci and said, *what Scribe has told you is completely true and exactly what will happen on the day my father chooses for this to come to pass. There is no doubt about what Scribe says and I know because my father has told me the same thing many times.* Nykloneci did not know what to think, how could someone who writes the exploits and the deeds of the servants of the king hold such a high honor and be given something like this to do?

Scribe spoke up and said, *it is not like you think, yes it will bring devastation to the land of the king but it will be what he wants to bring to pass. I don't do this on my own.*

Scribe continued telling Nykloneci that he had often sat and explained to the king that this honor and privilege should be reserved for his general who will be serving him at that time. The king was adamant that Scribe will be the one who will call forth the things which need to be set in place so the end can come.

Nykloneci began to understand what most people thought of as the most important jobs which needed to be done for the king were not nearly as important as the jobs most people took for granted. Here was a servant of the king going about his daily duty and writing in many books all that was happening in the kingdom so the complete and accurate records could be kept of everything that was done in service to the king.

Before he had time to think it through, Nykloneci looked at Scribe and asked him who was writing his book of service to the king. Scribe and Susthris both looked at each other and laughed so loud that they stopped and looked around the library to be sure nobody else was there to hear them. Scribe explained that what he did was recorded but not for anyone to see, it was kept in the secret place in the library. Nykloneci looked at Scribe and asked where this secret place was; he had been all over the library and had not seen any secret places. There were rows and rows of books all around the structure but he had not found any secret places.

THE BEGINNINGS OF NYKLONECI

Scribe looked at Nykloneci and said, *well I guess the secret places are still secret and you have not looked hard enough to find them here.*

Nykloneci had to admit he did not do a lot of walking around in the library. He mostly sat in one place, and Scribe had been the one who came to him and brought the next book for him to read. It was at this point Nykloneci realized that he had not treated Scribe very well. He just sat at a table and asked Scribe for the next book which he was supposed to read. He did not even take the time and energy to walk to the shelves and replace the book he had been reading and look for the next one himself. Scribe looked at Nykloneci and said, *it is okay; you have been my guest here for the past few months. I was instructed to assist you in every way possible and that is what I did. I wanted your time here to be pleasant, and I did all I could to help you in your searches through the books of the generals and the great servants of the king.*

It was at this point Nykloneci started thinking and asked why Scribe had not brought him any books about his father, the elder. Scribe said, *I have been working on his books, and they are not available to be read at this time. It will be fine for you to come back later, and I will get them for you. But now they are being used to fill in some of what he is working on for the king.*

Nykloneci then asked if it was possible for him to read any of the books that Scribe had written about himself. Scribe apologized and stated they were being written actively, too, so they were not available at this time either, but maybe later he could look them over when he got time. Susthris asked Nykloneci if there was anything else that he could answer for him now. Nykloneci asked, *what is the king like and could I ever meet him personally?* Susthris stated, *the king is like everyone* else. *There are things the king needs to do and places he needs to go, so he is not really much different than others in the kingdom.* He did say, as an afterthought, *the king is normally extremely busy and he rarely takes time to entertain anyone who is learning about the kingdom.*

Susthris quickly added, *one day soon, you will have the full attention of the king and he will be able to talk with you at length.* This shocked Nykloneci and he asked, *how do you know this and what does this mean?* Susthris would only say, *in time most of the loyal subjects of the king get time to spend with him to talk and interact with him on a personal level.* Susthris also said, *I need to get back to my father; we are scheduled to meet, and I need to be going on my way.* Susthris excused himself and left Nykloneci and Scribe in the library and hurried along on his way to the king.

When he reached the door and was ready to leave, he looked at Scribe and said, *you need to talk to my father about Nykloneci spending time with the Death Messenger. It would be a good experience for him, and it would help him to understand the kindness that my father shows to those who have served him well.* Scribe told Nykloneci, *this is an excellent idea and I will go at once and see what the king thinks of this opportunity.* He walked briskly to the door and was gone before Nykloneci had time to think about what had just transpired.

The thought of the Death Messenger brought a chill to Nykloneci. Anyone who knew anything realized that being around this one could be the beginning of their end. He was very concerned when he grasped the full impact of what Susthris had proposed to Scribe.

Nykloneci figured that Scribe would return with the king's answer, and it would be like everything else, denied. Most of his other requests had been brought back this way so he was sure this one would also be denied.

Scribe returned quickly to the library and picked up the books which he had been writing in and started working away on them. Nykloneci waited a few moments, and then he asked Scribe what the king had said about spending time with the Death Messenger. Scribe looked up from his work and said, *oh yes, the king thought Susthris had an excellent idea and you will go see him after you are done with the book that you are reading now.*

This answer shook Nykloneci to his very core and he wondered what this time would be like. He even began to wonder if he would be in danger of being carried off by the Death Messenger. He had heard so many stories about this one, and nobody wanted to be close to him or spend time around him; it was just too scary to think about. Scribe came by a few minutes later and asked Nykloneci how long it would take him to read the last chapter in the book he was on. Nykloneci said maybe he would get it done tomorrow when he came back to the library.

Scribe laughed and said, *you better hurry and get done. I can feel the Death Messenger coming to get you now. Can you feel the chill in the air and the sense of foreboding which is coming into the room here now? This is the way it feels when he comes to someone and I know the king has already sent for him to allow you time to join in his work. Finish the book as quickly as you can and be ready when he comes and stands before you.*

The Death Messenger

There was only one more servant of the king who needed to spend time with Nykloneci to help him to understand all that was required in serving the king. This was the one who King Hertfa sent out to keep watch over his servants. This one was given the honor and privilege of taking those who were about to pass from life to King Hertfa. When it was time for any of the servants of the king to pass from life, it was his duty to take them to the king and allow them to stand in his presence. This was an awesome task and one which was reserved for a special one of standing with the king.

Instead of being a terrible taskmaster as it was often supposed he was. This one was given the gift of seeing those who needed to come before the king and allow them to do so before their time in the land was over. This one was the one who was given the dark cloak of death to wear. He had the staff of collection placed in his hand to accomplish what the king needed to have done. The dynamic of this one was that he was greatly feared by all the inhabitants of the land. His very presence was enough to bring fear and trembling to all who encountered him as he traveled the land for King Hertfa.

The people of the land knew that once he passed by you, it was possible to glimpse him only for an instant, and if he came for you, there was no stopping him. The Death Messenger was given the task of collecting the people who were destined to die and take them to the king so he could pronounce judgment on them. His job was not a normal occurrence within the service of the king. He was feared and hated by most who did not understand his purpose and goal. His very presence made the air go cold, and when he came to visit anyone, they knew instantly who he was and what he was there for. Everyone knew when this servant of the king came to you it meant the end of your life.

Interestingly enough, many times he was only coming to see the progress people had made in their life. He was only passing through the land of the king to check on those who had accomplished great things for the king. But as is the case in most situations, the people did not understand his goal and his appearing. Fear and hatred ran deep with all the residents of the land of the king with regard to the Death Messenger.

When the Death Messenger would reveal himself to anyone, the first thing they would notice was the air had gone extremely cold. Once they made the connection this was a visit by him, they would proceed to try to run and hide from him, knowing this was impossible.

Many would say once he came to them, and most times it was only to check on their service to the king, that they could see his eyes beneath the cloak and this was the only prominent feature they could make out at first. The old ones always said, *his eyes glowed red, and once you saw them, your days were numbered.*

They did not realize or understand the kindness that he was trying to show them. It was truly a great and awesome honor for the Death Messenger to visit you without taking you to see King Hertfa. After it was apparent he was only there to check on their progress, many stated it was only after the initial shock of seeing this immense cloaked figure and the red eyes that they could see the collection staff.

If the staff was contained within his hands and it was not pointed at you, it was only a visit and a time of seeing your condition and progress for the king. But if you saw the Death Messenger pointing the staff of collection at you, your time was over in life. This shadowy approach and the way he turned the air to ice, this is what drew the attention to him as being a negative entity for the king.

Nobody realized how important it was for the Death Messenger to visit and spend time acknowledging them to the king. This was like having the seal of approval from King Hertfa for the Death Messenger to come and inspect your work and then return to report to the king.

The fear and trepidation which always accompanied his visit was enough for many to claim, once you were visited by the Death Messenger, your days were numbered. This became the omen for the people that once he placed his gaze on you, you would pass from life. A visit from the Death Messenger was an honor which was bestowed by the king so that your life was being shown as coming up before him as a remembrance. The Death Messenger was sent to those that King Hertfa wanted to show his approval and his understanding to.

For the most part, his mission was misunderstood by those who he visited. Once he came to them, they looked for death when they should have understood that it was a remembrance of their life. As is the case with so many things King Hertfa set in place, the people did not understand his intent or the purpose for the visits by the Death Messenger.

THE BEGINNINGS OF NYKLONECI

Since most did not understand the workings of the Death messenger, it was imperative that Nykloneci begin to grasp his purpose and the work he did. After Nykloneci had spent time with Gammy and Scribe, it was time for him to understand the workings of this servant of the king and accompany him on his rounds in the kingdom.

At first Nykloneci did not grasp or understand why he would need this part of his training. He felt like he was being punished for something because of his constant asking for time with the crafters. But it was only to balance his training and show him this very important aspect of service to King Hertfa.

Herbance had often worked with the Death Messenger. It was a common practice for him to accompany this servant to visit the subjects of the king. The importance was for those who served King Hertfa to know this person was coming to them to bring them back to reality and not think more highly of themselves than they should. These visits also served to help them to understand that someone was watching them as they did their service to King Hertfa. It allowed them to realize and understand their frailness with regard to life and living. Once the Death Messenger paid a visit to someone, they no longer took life for granted. They realized that many forces were at work in their lives and it helped them to be grateful for what they had and were able to do for the king.

Herbance had been helping with this process through the Death Messenger and would often accompany him on his rounds to see how things were progressing for the king. There were many times when he was traveling with the Death Messenger and because of his cloak, he would often be mistaken for him until the people realized that more than one servant of the king was visiting them.

The Death Messenger did come to those who had lived out their lives. It was his duty and responsibility to take them to the king once their time was over in life. This gave him the bad reputation of being an evil force instead of the positive worker that he was for the king.

You have to understand that it was a great honor and privilege for the Death Messenger to come and take you to the king when your time was over. The Death Messenger has many assistants who could come and take you to the king. So having the Death Messenger come to you and take you to the king directly, with all the people who needed to be taken, was a true honor. This was a privilege that was reserved for the most faithful servants of King Hertfa. Most people did not see it this way and this is what led to the negative connotation about the Death Messenger, but his service was true and faithfully executed for the king.

The fact it was possible for everyone he passed by to feel his presence and know he came near them only fed the belief that once he visited you, your time was short. This was not the case, and many times it was during his travels to collect others that he chose to stop by and see how other people were performing their service to the king.

Herbance was given the chance to see the kindness that the Death Messenger used to gather those who needed to go to the king. His countenance was like that of one who truly understood the value of someone to take them to the king. He was gentle with those he gathered, and he carried them to the king with care.

THE BEGINNINGS OF NYKLONECI

The Death Messenger was a special one that had to have some unique and wonderful qualities for him to be able to serve in this capacity. The Death Messenger had to have compassion for those people he carried to the king. Without this aspect of his makeup, the journey to the king would truly be a terrible one.

Nykloneci was given the chance to help the Death Messenger carry out his duties for the king. He did not understand why this was a needed aspect of his training, but he did assist in this capacity for a short period of time.

Nykloneci came into the presence of the Death Messenger in the library. He looked at him and wondered why so much fear was associated with him by so many people. All it took was for the Death Messenger to turn and allow Nykloneci to look into his red glowing eyes, and then he felt the fear so many had experienced.

There was just something about those eyes that made Nykloneci cringe and want to turn away and run and hide. Nykloneci was able to finally stop shaking and feeling this overwhelming fear after a short time. When the Death Messenger looked at him, he began to understand that his countenance did not display his gentle nature.

Nykloneci spent some time traveling with the Death Messenger and learning what he did and how he brought such fear to people. It was not his gentle nature that showed through to everyone, it was his appearing with his eyes blazing red and his large size that put people at such an uneasy state.

His appearance did not match the nature of him. But since most people did not understand what he did was a kindness and necessary requirement of the king, they only saw him as a menace to them. Nykloneci came to understand what the

Death Messenger did was not the menacing appearing and taking away loved ones. His assignment was allowing those about to pass from life to go to the king.

This was a totally new experience for Nykloneci and he did not fully grasp what this entailed. He did know that this servant who was doing this work was not trying to instill fear even though this was the normal outcome for anyone who saw him.

King Hertfa wanted everyone to know when this special servant came to someone before they passed from life. The effect of seeing the Death Messenger was something that was supposed to bring peace and harmony to the person who was ready to go to the king. Most of the people who are ready to go to the king feel this way about this one who comes to them and helps them go to the king.

The people who are not ready to go to the king because of their death are the ones who see the Death Messenger as something ominous and become fearful of him. King Hertfa never intended for those who are not ready to pass from their life to see this servant of his. But for some reason he is visible to most people no matter what their status in life.

Even with this knowledge, King Hertfa has never changed anything about the appearance and the ability of people to see the Death Messenger. It should be possible for the king to change his appearance or to block those who are not close to death, but for some reason this has never happened. It is almost as if the king knew there would be times when people needed to see this servant of his and help them to understand that life is precious.

Nykloneci realized quickly this servant was not a named one and that his title was what he was called. He thought it strange for someone with this kind of service to the king would not have a proper name which was used to address him.

Nykloneci thought about it for a while then he asked the Death Messenger, *what is your name?* The Death Messenger looked at Nykloneci with those red glowing eyes, and said, *my name is not important only the service that I do for the king is important.* Nykloneci gasped when he realized that this was the first time he had heard him speak and his voice was a low, raspy whisper instead of a strong, vibrant voice. Nykloneci pressed the Death Messenger to answer his question about his name. This is when the Death Messenger told him, *I am the third one to hold this position and both of my predecessors will not deal with mankind any longer.*

Nykloneci wondered what this meant so he asked him straightforwardly what this meant when all he had done was asked him his name. The Death messenger took the time to explain to Nykloneci that he was only the third being to hold this position and nobody had ever asked any of them what their name was. This puzzled Nykloneci, and he asked again, *what is your name so I can address you properly?* The Death Messenger looked at him again and stated, *my name for all practical purposes is the Death Messenger and this is all anyone needs to call me.* Nykloneci explained, *I was not trying to be disrespectful to you but everyone I have met or worked with so far has a name.* Nykloneci could not understand why this position would have someone that would not be named other than his position.

He took the time to explain to the Death Messenger that he had worked closely with Gammy and then Scribe and both of them had names. He even took the time to talk about Susthris and how he was the son of the king but he still had a name and it was normal to have a name. The Death Messenger looked at Nykloneci and said, *I do not have a need for a name, I am my position and that is enough.*

Confusion set in for Nykloneci, and he asked, *did you ever have a name before you accepted this position for the king?* At this the Death Messenger stopped and looked like he might be confused with this question. Nykloneci told the Death Messenger, *my name is Nykloneci and I have several nicknames people have given me over the years and they all apply to me too. All I am asking is for you to reveal your name to me so I will know what to call you.*

The Death Messenger made an attempt at laughter but all that came out was a willowy wisp of a sound. He looked at Nykloneci and said, *I do not understand why a name is so important when everyone knows who I am? All I have to do is appear to those who need to see me and immediately they know who I am and there is no doubt in their minds who is visiting them.*

Nykloneci asked again if he had a name before he took this position for King Hertfa and if he could remember what it was. The Death Messenger stood and thought for a few moments and then he stated, *I do have a name after all and I have not been called by any name for so long that I had actually forgotten I have a proper name.*

Nykloneci waited for what seemed like an eternity for him before he finally asked again what his name was. He was shocked and amazed at the same time to hear one word being spoken by this raspy whisper of a voice. *Razielle,* was all that the Death Messenger spoke, and then he fell silent again. Nykloneci asked, *would it be possible for me to call you Razielle from now on or do you prefer the Death Messenger as your title and name?* Another few moments passed before the

Death Messenger answered, *it might be nice to be called by my proper given name again since it has been so long since I have heard it from anyone.* The rest of the time Nykloneci spent with Razielle was interesting and informative for him. He saw the kindness which was shown to the king's servants, and he also saw a change in Razielle.

The second day as they were traveling throughout the kingdom a blind man was standing on the road. Razielle stopped and stood in front of this man, and the man began to quake with fear. Nykloneci told the blind man his name and asked him why he was so afraid. The blind man told Nykloneci, *I am afraid but even though I am blind I can see two red eyes burning in front of me.* Nykloneci asked, *how can you see two red eyes if you are blind?* The man stated, *the eyes appeared in my mind and not in front of my blind eyes. This is how I am able to see them.*

This amazed Nykloneci and he told the man he was correct but the eyes he saw did not belong to him but to the Death Messenger. With this statement the man became overjoyed and revealed that he had been looking for him for years, he was ready to go to the king and be judged. The Death Messenger came to this man's side and held his arm and escorted him gently to the king. After the blind man had been taken to King Hertfa, Razielle asked Nykloneci, *do you truly understand why it is necessary for me to take people to the king?* Nykloneci stated that it was important for people to be taken to the king and this was his job and position in his service to the king.

Razielle looked at Nykloneci and said, *yes, what you say is true, but do you understand why this is necessary?* Nykloneci did not know how to answer this because he knew what Razielle did was important but he did not truly understand why it needed to be done. Nykloneci admitted that he did not understand why this needed to be done and could it be explained to him so he would know why this service was needed.

Razielle told Nykloneci about the first Death Messenger and how King Hertfa knew mankind was a confused and disoriented lot. King Hertfa understood many of the humans who had died up to this point did not know that they were dead.

Razielle said, *before there was a Death Messenger, many of the humans walked the realm thinking they were just feeling a bit off that day instead of realizing they had died. This led to many problems because as they walked along they would talk to the other people around them and then get upset when nobody ever answered them. After a short time of this they would become violent and try to injury the people that they came into contact with, and this led to many problems for the living.*

King Hertfa realized this had to stop so he asked his servants if any of them would be willing to help mankind to come to him when they died so they did not try to hurt the people around them. The first Death Messenger stood up and told the king that he was willing to help them and bring them to him so he could judge them and explain what had happened to them.

After this process was established, those people who were close to death would be sought out by the Death Messenger and taken to the king. Within a short time the Death Messenger went to the king and explained that he did not realize how many men and women were dying daily. The king's realm covered a large area, and it was almost impossible for him to bring all the ones who approached death to the king.

King Hertfa agreed that this was not the task for one being so he asked the Death Messenger how many others he needed to assist him. The decision was made and the Death Messenger approached the king with a specific number that it would take to assist him and that number was eighty-one. The king was overwhelmed to realize that it would take that many to assist the Death Messenger, so he changed the number to twenty-seven. The Death Messenger then asked the king what the circumstances were that needed to come to pass before he could send one of the others to assist those about to die and take them to the king.

King Hertfa did not hesitate with his answer and he explained and expressed that those people in his kingdom who had been faithful and supportive to his wishes would require the Death Messenger to assist them in coming to him. The other people in his empire who did not support the king could be helped by his assistants. This was agreed upon by the king and the Death Messenger and this set the standard for how it worked at that time. Anyone who has been faithful to King Hertfa would be assisted by the Death Messenger and anyone else could be helped by one of his twenty-seven assistants.

The problem appeared to be solved, and the work began for the Death Messenger and his helpers. During the course of time, the Death Messenger realized there were many problems with what he had agreed to do for the king. As time passed he realized that taking on this position for the king was a mistake which he could not undo or change.

The first Death Messenger learned to hate mankind, and he came to realize that his task would never be done. If he was able to catch up one day, the next day more would need to be gathered and taken to King Hertfa. It was still questionable about which people he would need to gather and which ones he could send his assistants to gather. Most times he needed to go talk to the king about which ones he needed to collect and bring to him.

Sometimes he was not able to go to the king when things were planned, and he could not interrupt when ceremonies were going on. When this happened he would often go to Scribe and ask him about who he should collect and who he could send his assistants to gather.

Scribe could access the books in the library and let the first Death Messenger know which ones he needed to get and which ones he was able to send his workers to get, but this created problems that nobody foresaw.

It was only after several years that the first Death Messenger was able to maintain his position and provide this service to the king. Once he reached the end of his ability to tolerate the humans, he went to the king and begged to be removed from this position for the king.

King Hertfa realized he had put the first Death Messenger in a position that he would never want anything to do with mankind again. King Hertfa appointed him a position that would allow him to refrain from human contact again and still allowed him to serve him in a special way.

The search began for the next Death Messenger. This one knew what he was up against before he took this position of showing kindness to mankind.

The second Death Messenger worked well within the system that King Hertfa set up, but he insisted on having the eighty one helpers to get everything accomplished the way the king desired. He also made it plain to the king that there would be a group of ten assistants who could get anyone for the king instead of the Death Messenger alone.

King Hertfa finally realized that what he had expected from this position was just too much for one being to handle. King Hertfa accepted this implementation and allowed it to become the standard. It was agreed between the second Death Messenger and *the king that he would still go to get the most loyal subjects of King Hertfa whenever possible.*

But there would be times when one of his ten assistants would be required to bring some of the faithful ones to the king for their judgment. This would only happen when there were several people who were ready to pass from life at the same time. These new changes were made and became the new standard which is still in effect today.

King Hertfa reluctantly agreed to this stipulation and understood that there would be times when several of his most faithful ones would need to be brought to him at the same time. It was also decided that whenever possible the king would give prior instructions as to which person the Death Messenger was to get and bring to the king before it became a dire situation. This worked relatively well for many years, and the second Death Messenger carried out his duties with accuracy and with compassion toward the humans who he brought to King Hertfa.

The only problem arose when it was considered to be unfair with the treatment the king gave to the humans compared to the other beings in his realm. This issue arose after many years of faithful service by the second Death Messenger and his service would have continued for a longer period if only this issue was not realized and discussed by many of the other beings.

This became a problem area within a few years, and the second Death Messenger realized there was no equality in the treatment between the humans and the other beings. This prompted the second Death Messenger to decide that his time of service to the king in this capacity was drawing to a close. He approached King Hertfa with this complaint and admitted that it was causing him problems after all of these years whenever he had to deal with the humans and see the special considerations which they were given.

King Hertfa listened to his complaint and agreed that maybe it was time for him to serve in another capacity and it would be wise to replace him as quickly as possible. It was decided to do another search for someone who would gladly and lovingly take this position and carry out all of the king's desires.

The opportunity was presented to the servants closest to the king, but none of them were willing to accept this position from the king. They all agreed that it would take a special one to handle this point of service to the king. A search was made, and nobody was found who wanted this position within the realm of the king.

The king began to wonder if the stress and constant service was too much to ask until someone mentioned that those who used to serve the king might be a better fit for this work. King Hertfa thought about this proposal for a short time and he pondered the effects of allowing this to come to pass.

If he was willing to allow one being who used to be a faithful servant, but was not one now, to take this position would there be problems that would arise from doing this? It was time to consult his closest and most trusted servants, and the king called in all of his elders to consult with them about this matter.

The day came when all the elders and those in positions of authority to the king met to discuss this issue and to weigh the results of such a plan. After a few days of deliberations and constant questions and rebuttals, it was decided that this approach would open the door for a new opportunity which never existed before.

Herbance was quick to explain that this would be a wonderful opportunity which must not be missed by this group. The king took their advice and this position of support and help to the king was presented to those in the eleventh dimensional realm.

This had never been presented to those who used to serve the king but now were not, and it was wondered if it could be a real

THE BEGINNINGS OF NYKLONECI

opportunity by those in the eleventh dimensional realm. King Hertfa went into the eleventh realm and presented this line of thinking and waited to see if anyone would respond to this call back into the service of the king.

There was only one who answered the king with an immediate yes. Razielle was the only one in this realm to grab the opportunity and go forward in it. This was how I, Razielle came to be the third Death Messenger.

The reason I was given this opportunity was because I knew that if the king allowed this to come to pass, his compassion and mercy would be a constant reminder to me while I was taking those in need to the king. I was given the chance which nobody had ever been given before. I gladly accepted and saw my service to the king with the eyes of one who was shown mercy beyond what I deserved. I knew I would always be able to look with eyes of compassion on every human that I took to see the king for their judgment.

When Razielle finished this story to Nykloneci and looked at him, something very dramatic happened. As Nykloneci was looking into his red eyes, they suddenly began to glow orange.

It was at this point that Nykloneci knew he had just heard more from this poor creature about the mercy of the king than he had ever heard before. When Razielle looked at anyone who needed to be taken to the king, his eyes showed as a pair of red glowing orbs. But since he had shared his secret with Nykloneci and had trusted him enough to share this story, his eyes always glowed orange when he looked at Nykloneci. This sparked an idea in Nykloneci that he knew one day he would bring to pass and when his time came, he would be ready to fulfill his destiny.

He now knew what he needed to do in his service to King Hertfa, and it was as if the puzzle of his life was finally starting to take shape and form. He understood for the first time with a complete realization of what his future service would be. Now he knew without any doubt that he would be able to one day fulfill his calling to the king.

Lustureus was standing in the shadows as this story was revealed to Nykloneci. Lustureus realized that the time for his control of Nykloneci was growing closer with each new day. He now knew exactly how he would implement his plan in the life of Nykloneci. He now knew what he needed to do to gain control of him and make him his slave.

Afterword

We all have things that we must face in life, and we all know the day will come when we realize this firsthand. Coming to the place of understanding that we are not always the one in control of our life will be monumental for us. There are times when things just happen. There are also times when things happen for a reason. There will be other times when things happen because of the influence and direction of others around us. It is imperative we begin to understand that some decisions are made for us and others we get to pick and choose. Some parts of our lives are under the direct control of others and some of us just make the bad decisions most of the time. But there are times when we are under the dark lord's power without realizing that they are influencing our lives and causing the issues which come into our lives. Many times we say our luck is bad, but in reality, there are forces at work in our lives that we do not realize or understand. Just like Nykloneci, we all have times when things are directed and laid out for us. We go along thinking and hoping that we are following the right way. Learn more about Nykloneci and his life by delving into the next edition of the Nykloneci series. You will learn how we are all under the control and direction of the dark lords at times. Look for *The Rise of Nykloneci in His Service to the King* as the next installment in this series. Enjoy!